THE UPSIDE TO BEING SINGLE

EMMA HART

NEW YORK TIMES BESTSELLING AUTHOR

Cover Design and Formatting by Emma Hart
Editing by Ellie at LoveNBooks

For Darryl.
It takes an incredible person to love a writer. It takes an
even more special one to understand them.

THE UPSIDE TO BEING SINGLE

UPSIDE #1: YOU CAN BUY THE TOILET PAPER YOU LIKE.

"There are penises everywhere!" The woman in her late sixties who'd been the bane of my existence since she'd checked in three days ago covered the eyes of her seven-year-old granddaughter.

Obviously, she was ignoring the fact boobs were also everywhere and hadn't bothered to cover the eyes of the twelve-year-old boy who was currently looking around the small lobby like a kid seeing Disney World for the first time.

I really didn't have the time nor the patience for this lady's fifteen-thousandth complaint.

More to the point: she'd brought her grandkids to Mardi Gras.

Mardi.

Freaking.

Gras.

What was she expecting? Sunshine and rainbows and kittens? I mean, sure, there were probably a few of those around the parades—who the hell knew?—but that wasn't the point.

I was born and raised in New Orleans, and Mardi Gras was the last place I would take my kids for a vacation.

Honestly, I was tired. I was fed up. I'd fought endless complaints from fussy customers. I'd been in a fight with the liquor company. I'd called an ambulance because someone had a panic attack and couldn't breathe, and to top it off, it was day one of freaking shark week.

That's right. Not only did I have to deal with a woman who didn't research her week's break for her grandkids, I was basically pissing blood as I tried to keep my temper.

Have you ever tried to keep your temper on your period?

Don't.

Just... Don't do that to yourself.

I wasn't one for stellar advice, but that? Gold. Pure gold. Trust me.

I took a deep breath before I addressed her. "Ma'am, it's Mardi Gras. Unfortunately, we aren't responsible for what happens during the festival."

"Could you not ask them—Johnny! Stop staring at those women!" She finally grabbed hold of the pre-teen and pulled him against her.

He spun his head as far as it would go until she gave him a quick clip around the back of the head.

I didn't want to judge but...you brought him here, lady.

Finally having the pre-teen under control, she returned her attention to me.

Oh, goodie.

"The website didn't state we'd be visiting the city during a time of such debauchery."

Cute. She thought this was Buckingham Palace or something.

I plastered my reassuring customer-service look on my face. Wide, pitying eyes. A sympathetic curl of my lips... A heavy lean on my deep, Southern accent. "Ma'am, I'm real sorry y'all aren't having the trip y'all imagined, but it's not the hotel's job to do more than inform potential guests of events ahead of time. I'm sure you appreciate that we can't control

Mardi Gras or what people do while here, and we do advise in the Frequently Asked Question section of the website that guests visiting with children avoid Mardi Gras unless traveling here is absolutely necessary."

She sniffed, tilting her chin upward. "I'd like to speak to the manager, please."

"You already are, ma'am."

"You're the manager?"

"Yes."

If it was possible, her expression darkened. "I'd like to inform you that we'll be checking out later today."

"Awww," said the pre-teen boy.

"But, Grandma, we have three more sleeps. You said so!" The little girl tugged on her arm.

She gently removed the little girl's hand from her arm and shushed her softly, then turned back to me. "I trust we'll be able to receive a refund."

"Actually…"

"I don't like how you're beginning that sentence, Miss…"

"Rogers," I said. I schooled my expression once more into something…well, something that didn't show her my annoyance. "I'll need your full name to check your booking on the system."

"Mrs. Catherine Reynolds."

I typed her name into the system, and her booking came up instantly. After I clicked on it, I scanned over it. "I'm sorry, Mrs. Reynolds. A refund isn't possible."

"Isn't possible? Why not?"

"You booked on our super-saver rate, and even if you hadn't, reservations must be canceled forty-eight hours before arrival, per the terms on the website."

"I'm not canceling a reservation; I'm leaving early. I'd like a refund for the three nights I won't be here."

What part of "a refund wasn't possible" was she not understanding?

"Unfortunately, the chance of us being able to fill your room is very slim. Our terms state refunds for early check-outs are only applicable in limited instances. Leaving because you aren't happy with the city isn't one of those."

Whoops. That came out a little bitchy.

"I'm very sorry," I continued. "You are welcome to leave, but we're unable to refund you for the remainder of your stay."

She pursed her lips. "I will be complaining to your boss about this as soon as I'm home."

She could have fun with that. I didn't even know the name of my new boss. Nobody had bothered to tell me yet, and I doubt I'd know until he showed up in two days.

"I'm very sorry you had a bad experience with us, Mrs. Reynolds."

"Not sorry enough to offer me a refund. Come on, kids." She sniffed and walked off once again, and I muttered under my breath when she'd disappeared.

Somebody really needed to make a PSA about Mardi Gras. Maybe I'd put a pop-up screen on the website warning people it's not exactly kid-friendly.

Ugh…

"I'm here! Sorry! I got caught by the damn barricades going up." Lillie slid up to me in reception with a sheepish smile. "Are you mad?"

"Did you bring me food?"

She raised a brown paper bag and a Starbucks mug. "One Berry Refresher doohickey and a cream cheese and salmon bagel from that place you like."

I took both from her. "That almost soothes the sting from my encounter with Mrs. Reynolds."

She winced, tucking loose strands of her raven hair behind her ear. "Ouch. What was it this time?"

I glanced at the bustling lobby. "Well, the good news is that she's leaving early."

"That means there's bad news."

I nodded. "She'll be complaining to the new owner before he even steps foot in the hotel."

"Oh, good," she drawled, taking over the space on reception. "Is she going to come down here with her saggy guns blazing, or will she go quietly?"

"Judging by the way she had to usher her kids out, she might go quietly, but they sure as hell won't."

"Oh God. Have I told you how much I hate you for leaving me to deal with this?"

"No, but I'd advise against it. I'm still in charge." I grinned, backing toward the staff area. "And no refunds, Lil. I mean it. Under no circumstances to her."

She gave me a mock-salute and stood to mock-attention. "Yes, ma'am."

"Call me that again, and you're fired."

"I love you so much."

I nodded toward the young couple walking in the direction of the reception desk. "Do your job, you little suck up."

She laughed.

I left, drink and lunch in hand.

Today was for the birds.

—◦•◦—

Peyton peered at me over the rim of her cocktail glass. "That bad?"

I nodded. "She came back down and complained to Lillie for an hour. An hour."

Chloe screwed up her face. "Why didn't she just call the cops? They've dealt with unruly customers for you before."

"Drunk customers," I corrected her. "Not sixty-whatever grandmas with their grandkids in tow."

"Imagine complaining about the number of penises," Peyton mused, tucking her dark-brown hair behind her ear. "Was she a nun?"

I drained the rest of my drink and shrugged. "Whatever she was, she was an idiot. She hadn't done a second of research. Was she expecting Mickey fucking Mouse to pop out mid-parade?"

"Maybe. It wouldn't be the first time."

Chloe snorted, clapping her hand over her mouth. It didn't work. Her cocktail spurted out of her nose anyway.

Peyton and I both burst out laughing as she wiped her mouth.

"Screw you both," Chloe said. "I was just thinking about that time in senior year when we did the Homecoming Parade and Danny Johnson jumped out dressed as Mickey."

Peyton wrinkled up her face. "That was humiliating."

"Only because he kissed you…Still wearing the Mickey head."

"Do you have to remind me of that all the time? We weren't even dating."

"No," I said, "but you were texting him while you were dating Callum Deveraux."

"Look here." Peyton gripped her glass with one hand and held up her forefinger on the other. "That was not what happened, and you know it."

"Peyt," Chloe began. "That's exactly what happened."

She twirled her hair around her finger. "I mean, not exactly. I was kinda broken up with Callum."

"We're not doing the 'on a break' thing." I waggled my finger at her. "It didn't work for Ross, and it won't work for you."

"I'm not Rachel! We were on a break. Do I need to call my phone company and get the damn text message record?"

"Do they keep them this long?"

"I don't know, but I'd try it to prove you assholes wrong." She downed the last of her cocktail and slammed the glass on the table. A tiny bit of moisture lingered on her chin from the icy glass, and she reached to wipe it away with her hand. "When did this turn into a slamming Peyton session?"

Chloe paused. "I don't know, but it's fun."

"I hate you." Peyton pouted, but there was laughter in her eyes. "Are y'all ready to leave?"

Chloe finished her drink and nodded, waving to get the attention of our server. Getting it, she signaled for the check and turned back to us. "Ready?" she asked, her dark eyes glancing over both of us.

We nodded, and the server brought the check in record-fast time. We all laid down the cash for our dinner—we'd learned long ago that charging three cards takes forever, especially during Mardi Gras. Grabbing our things, I gave a final, if tipsy, sweep of the table with my eyes and followed my best friends to the stairs and through the downstairs level of the restaurant.

The humid spring air hit us with a shudder. It didn't matter that we'd lived here our whole lives—the shock of stepping from a cool, air-conditioned place into the sticky-aired street would never change.

"Let's get a drink." Peyton grabbed both of our arms and drug us toward the nearest cocktail store on the corner of the street.

"No," I groaned. "I have to work tomorrow."

"Since when did that stop you?" Her taunt was accompanied by a wide grin and a twinkle in her eyes.

"I have to work tomorrow, too," Chloe said hesitantly.

That stopped Peyt in her tracks. "You own a dating website. You can literally work while you take a shit in the morning."

"She has a point," I admitted, "I, however, have to deal with people who complain about the size of the complimentary shampoo bottles in their bathrooms."

"People complain about that?" Peyton asked. "Really? I'm just glad to get the free shampoo."

"And she'll never let you book a room at her hotel," Chloe said for me. "One drink, Peyton, and not one the length of my torso."

Peyt grinned and clapped her hands together.

Our first mistake was letting her into the cocktail bar by herself.

Our second mistake was not being able to look through the window.

Our third mistake? Taking the torso-length, plastic cocktail glasses shaped like palm trees and letting her shout "no backsies!" like a fucking twelve-year-old.

There was a reason Peyton Austin owned the only hook-up website in Louisiana. She was the girl-next-door—the party chick with a bookish streak. A complete and utter enigma.

She understood everyone...

Except her best friends who said no.

One day. One day, we would get her so drunk, she'd learn her lesson.

Today was not that day.

I sipped the frozen mango margarita. I couldn't be mad. She'd gotten my favorite cocktail, after all, and it looked like Chloe was having the same issue with her drink.

The sip, swallow, sigh gave it all away.

Nothing good would come of this.

UPSIDE #2: YOU DON'T HAVE TO WEAR A PRETTY BRA TO IMPRESS ANYONE. OR ANY BRA AT ALL.

I was right.

Three huge, frozen cocktails later, and we were wandering down the middle of Bourbon Street. Which was how I knew Chloe was drunk—she avoided this place as much as humanly possible.

Peyton was going to be in big trouble tomorrow.

Never mind them, though. They could work on their phones in bed. I was the only one who had to actually people. So why was I also a little past tipsy?

I was weak. And Peyton was a pusher.

No excuses.

Chloe sighed happily, clutching her huge cup with the remnants of her cocktail in it. "I feel old."

"Old? We're twenty-seven. We're not old." I snorted.

"I know, but look at all these twenty-one-year-olds."

We all paused as one of said twenty-one-year-olds flashed her boobs and promptly tripped over a drain covering.

"I sure as hell can't wear stripper shoes like that anymore," Peyton agreed. "What are they? Six inches?"

"Bigger than the cock of the guy pulling her up," I noted, watching as she brushed him off and flashed a grin at the guy who threw beads down at her.

"We should flash for beads. We haven't done that in a long time." Chloe grinned, clutching her straw between her teeth.

I raised an eyebrow. "Have we ever done that?"

Both of my best friends nodded.

I paused. "Uh, just me, then?"

"You've never flashed anyone for beads?" Peyton stopped in the middle of the street and stared at me.

"It's hardly shocking," I said. "Most other adult humans haven't either. And why would I? I can buy some on the corner."

Chloe shook her head, sipping. "Nope." She pointed the stupid cup at me. "Before you go home tonight, you're flashing someone."

"I'm not!"

Peyt grabbed me, her eyes sparkling under the bright lights. "You are. I dare you to."

Fuck it. She had me there. There was one thing I'd never been able to back down from, and that was a dare. I had no choice. I had to do it.

"Couldn't I just do it here, in the middle of the street, next to the group of drunken pirates trying to pull a couple of chicks dressed like fairies?" I asked.

"No." Peyton shook her head decisively.

Chloe shook hers, too, but stopped and put her hand on her head. Our taxi home would be detouring past her house first then...

"Why not?"

"Because if you're going to flash, you need to get something for it."

"That's one step closer to prostitution than I'd like to take." I chewed the inside of my lip. I knew she owned a hookup website, but geez...

"The guys on balconies don't buy beads to decorate their houses with. They buy them so idiots like us flash them. Ready? See them up there? Let me show you how easy it is." Chloe—who was one hundred percent hammered at this point—shoved her cup at me and walked a few feet through the crowds to where a guy was smoking on the balcony.

She got his attention with a wave and motioned around her neck.

He grinned.

God, he looked about twelve.

Without a care in the world, Chloe grabbed the bottom of her shirt and pulled it up.

Of course, she didn't care.

She was wearing a bra.

Me? I was not. I had expected a nice, quiet dinner, not a potential audition to become a stripper.

Oy vey... what was I doing?

"I'm not wearing a bra," I blurted to Peyton while Chloe caught... "Is that a paper airplane?"

Chloe hooked the beads around her neck and came back to us. "He just paper airplaned me his phone number. Like grabbed it from the table and threw it."

"That's kinda smooth," I admitted.

"But you're not going to call him," Peyton reminded her. "Since you're hopelessly in love with my brother."

"I am not hopelessly in love with your brother!"

"We're not having this conversation again. We all know you're in love with Dom, so get over it. Can we go now?" What? I'd take advantage of this change in conversation if it meant I could get out of this dare.

They both shook their heads. "Nope. You're going to flash someone, and you're going to do it right now."

"Not wearing a bra!"

"Even better," Chloe said. "You might get laid as well as beads."

"I should already be at home. In bed. For work tomorrow." I was such a party pooper. Also: a responsible adult. Most of the time.

Peyt grabbed my hand. "One flash. Ten seconds. Then I promise, I will hail us a cab and go home."

I was going to regret this. "Fine. But you have literally ten seconds to find someone for me to flash at, or I'm out of here."

On those words, she quite literally dragged me down the street, her eyes searching left and right for a balcony where I could lose my dignity.

"That one. Right there." She pointed to a balcony where four guys were sitting. They were older than the possibly-legal guy Chloe had just flashed. Not much older than us by the looks of it, but it was dark, and the lighting wasn't exactly LED bright, so who knew?

One of the guys leaned over the balcony and shouted something. I didn't know what it was, but Peyton obviously heard him, because she shouted back, "What have you got? We're not all wearing bras!"

Oh, Jesus.

I took a step back, but Chloe stuck her finger in the middle of my spine, moving me forward. I couldn't hear the rest of the conversation, but my eyes scanned the balcony. They were all good looking. One with dirty-blonde hair and blue eyes. Another with what seemed like jet-black hair and equally dark eyes. One who had his back to me.

And the guy in the corner.

No kidding, my clit danced a little bit for joy.

All right, so there was the part of me that'd already sacrificed its dignity.

Dark, wavy hair that was swept to one side and back. A sharp jaw that was dotted with dark stubble, just enough that it would tickle if you brushed your fingers over it.

His piercing gray eyes found mine, holding my gaze hostage for a moment before full lips curved into a smirk so daring and sexy I was ready to go spidergirl and climb up there to lick it right off his handsome face.

Well, all right. If I wanted to do that, I could flash. Right? Right.

Chloe nudged me. "Triple flash. Ready?"

"Yes." No. Never. Not ever.

Wasn't there another way to reclaim our youth? Like, oh, act our ages?

"One, two, three."

I did it. All that was holy, I grabbed the bottom of my shirt, looked Mr. Tall, Dark, and Silent in the eye, and flashed my bra-less boobs for the entire city to see.

Fine. Not the entire city, but it felt like it.

Thank God this city was already a pool of sin.

Mr. TDS—because Tall, Dark, and Silent was just way too long to keep saying, even inside my head—twitched his lips upward, grabbed something off the table, and tossed it my way.

A tiny shot bottle of Fireball.

Great.

That was all my dignity was worth.

I'd just flashed for Fireball.

I uncapped the bottle and downed it in one. Maybe it'd help me forget.

Lord, no. Nothing would help me forget this.

Chloe tossed a string of beads around my neck. "See? That wasn't so bad."

"I don't know," Peyton said. "She looks pretty traumatized."

Stopping in the middle of the street, enough of a distance away from the balcony with the hot guys, I stared at both of them. "You're both dead to me."

They burst out laughing.

"Think about it this way," Peyton said, linking her arm through mine and handing me my empty, giant cup. "You never have to see them again. You wouldn't recognize them at an empty bus stop."

Yeah, well, if she was wrong, I was going to kill her.

———o·•·o———

"The elevator is behind the reception counter and to your left. You're floor three, room six." Lillie slid a card-sized folder across the counter. "Thank you and enjoy your stay." She smiled her brightest smile at the customer who'd just taken the keycard from her and stayed in that perfectly poised position until the new check-in had headed for the elevators.

"All okay?" I asked, leaning against the side of the counter.

She nodded. "How are you feeling today? Better than yesterday when you had paperwork to do?" A knowing glint flickered in her eyes.

I held up my finger. "First, I did have paperwork to do. I also had a very important cat nap to take."

Lillie laughed.

"And yes, I'm fine. No more hangover. Which is just as well, because it's Monday, and the new owner is coming in to meet everyone today."

She wrinkled up her face. "Do you know anything about him?"

I smacked my lips together. "I finally know his name since he emailed me last night to tell me what time he'd be here today. Jacob Creed. Other than that, not a thing."

"He sounds old."

I rolled my eyes. "Yeah, well, he'll be here in about thirty minutes, no matter his age. I have to get the order in, so I'm going to see Harley to make sure she hasn't messed up the bar one again."

Lillie winced. "Right. Quinn is on vacation."

"I want her back already," I muttered. "If I don't come back by the time Mr. Creed arrives, get one of the bell guys to take him to my office and come get me from the storeroom. I'll be counting vodka and wishing I could drown in it."

"I see you learned a lot from your hangover."

I put my finger to my lips and pushed off the counter. I headed for the bar where I could already see Harley zipping back and forth. It was barely lunchtime, and it was already getting packed. The hotel was small, but the drinks were marginally cheaper than some of the bars, so we packed out quickly with people starting early.

Catching Harley between customers, I slipped behind the bar and pulled her to the side with an apology. "Did you do the order this morning?"

She took a deep breath.

That was reassuring.

"I did."

"Is it correct?"

"I think so."

"In other words, you need me to go to the storeroom and check it over."

She grimaced. "Please? Quinn changed some of the brands, and I'm still getting used to them."

For a mixologist-in-training, she was a few colors short of a rainbow, this one.

"All right. Where's the form? And is everything in the bar done?"

"Yes! And it's right here." She pulled it out from the cupboard. "Quinn sorted the bar and stocked it before she went, so I know it's all good."

It better have been.

"Okay. Thanks. I'll go and do this." I left the bar, swung through into the kitchen to get the chef's order form, and took both books into the chilly storeroom.

A shiver rippled across my skin at the cooler air, but I quickly got accustomed to the temperature and got to work on the bar order. I scanned gins, vodkas, fruity liquors… More bottles than I ever cared to pay attention to. They all blurred into one as I sighed and made my way through it.

Let's just say it was a good thing I was here to check it.

I was almost done when a glint of a blue bottle caught my eye. It was on the floor, rolled under the very bottom shelf. With another heavy sigh, I tugged my skirt up over my knees and got down onto them to get it, crawling beneath the shelf to grab it.

If it was broken, I'd lose my shit.

A throat cleared from somewhere behind me.

I jerked, banging the back of my head on the wooden shelf above me. "Shit! Oh, hell!" I grabbed the thankfully unsmashed bottle and crawled back out. "I'm sorry," I said, clearing the shelf.

"Mellie Rogers? The manager?"

That sounded like I was in trouble.

"That's me." I stood up and turned, clutching the bottle of Bombay Sapphire gin with one hand and doing my best at straightening my skirt at the same time.

"Jacob Creed. I'm the new owner. The girl at the front said you were here."

I looked up from my skirt and—

Oh no.

No, no, no.

I knew that dark, wavy hair. And that jaw. And those lips. And I definitely knew those gray eyes.

Because I'd looked into them as I'd flashed my boobs not even forty-eight hours earlier.

I was going to fucking kill Peyton Austin and Chloe Collins.

THREE

UPSIDE #3: THERE'S ALMOST NEVER A COMMITMENT TO THE PEOPLE WHO HAVE SEEN YOUR TATAS. *ALMOST.*

"Oh, fuck."

The words escaped me before I could stop them—and so did the bottle of gin. It slid right out of my grip and shattered as it made contact with the cold, concrete floor. I jumped back, away from the mess I'd just created, but I was almost numb to it. Any other day, I'd be rushing to clean it up.

Now, I left it. Left the glass to glint in the glaring overhead lights and the gin to trickle between the slightly uneven ridges in the floor.

How was this possible? How was Mr. Tall, Dark, and Silent standing in front of me?

This wasn't supposed to happen. I was never supposed to see him again. And now the universe was telling me his name was Jacob Creed—the hotel's new owner and my new boss?

No, no, no.

I was hungover. Daydreaming. In a nightmare. There was absolutely no way this was real. It couldn't be.

And in the space of five minutes, no matter what this was, I'd banged my head, sworn, and smashed a bottle of alcohol.

Good going, Mellie.

"I mean. Hi. I was just rescuing this." I pointed at the shattered bottle. "It fell. Rolled. Apparently, a pointless rescue."

His lips were pulled into that same smirk they'd formed on Saturday night, and his gray eyes glinted almost silver as he stepped forward and the light hit them. "Come away from that glass. Is there someone who can clean it up?"

"There's a broom…somewhere." Dazed. I was dazed. Shit.

Gray eyes scanned the room lighting up when they landed on the broom. He grabbed it and moved to sweep up most of the glass, pausing only to pick up what was left intact of the bottle.

I watched like an idiot until he was done and all that remained was a wet patch of wasted gin.

"Is your head okay?"

"My head?" I blinked at him.

He rubbed his hand over his jaw. "You just banged it on the shelf."

Oh my God, I did.

"It's…" I felt the back of my head. "A lump. It's fine. It'll go down."

"Here, let me see."

I giggled nervously and stepped back. "No, really, it's fine. It's not big. Just a small one." I clapped my hand over the back of my head, but if his step forward was any indication, he wasn't taking no for an answer.

"Please, let me check. Just in case it should be iced."

I took a deep breath and slowly let my hand fall to my side. "Fine."

He stepped behind me and gently parted my hair. I fought the urge to give into the shiver that wanted to tickle its way down my spine as he softly ran his fingertips over my scalp.

Why did that feel so good?

Why was I thinking this? Didn't I have enough to worry about now?

"I think that needs some ice. Just in case." He let my hair fall back into place and walked around to face me. "Do you feel okay? No dizziness or anything?"

"Does embarrassed count as okay?"

"I'd say that depends on the cause of the embarrassment." His eyes sparkled with silent laughter.

Yep. There went any hope it'd been too dark for him to see my face.

"I think I'll go and get that ice." I picked up the order books and, with my cheeks burning, grabbed the keys. He followed me out, and I locked the door, checked it, and glanced at him. "I'm sorry about that. You were supposed to be taken to my office."

He shrugged a shoulder and adjusted the sleeve of his jacket. "The bell guys were all busy, and the girl on reception didn't want me hanging around, so she sent me back here."

"Lillie. The reception girl." I glanced at him. "Well, I'm sorry. She should have taken you to the staff area, at least."

"It's fine. I didn't get lost. Which, for someone who got banned from going to the grocery store as a child because of that reason, is a pretty damn good feat."

My lips twitched into something that resembled a smile. My head was feeling damn sore.

"Hey, Lil, do we have ice packs anywhere?" I asked.

She glanced at Mr. TDS behind me.

Could I call him that now? Hmm.

"I'm not sure. There might be some in the kitchen. Why?"

"My fault," Mr. TDS jumped in with a raise of his hand. "She was getting a bottle that had rolled under the shelves, and instead of waiting, I distracted her, and she hit her head. She needs to ice it."

"Actually, I'm fine. It's fine," I said. Who was I reassuring? Probably myself, because that throbbing was growing.

"You're not fine. That's one hell of a lump." Mr. TDS looked at me firmly. "You need to ice it and sit down."

Lillie fought a smile. "Brittany's about to get off her break in a few minutes. Why don't y'all go to the office, and I'll have her bring one down to you when she's back?"

"Fine. Sure. Thank you." I forced a smile. "Oh, Lillie, this is Jacob Creed. Mr. Creed, this is Lillie. She's head of reception."

They shared a handshake.

"Pleasure to meet you, Mr. Creed. I promise she's not usually this clumsy," Lillie quipped.

"Pleasure is all mine, Lillie. That ice pack would be great, as soon as possible. Oh—and there's a little gin on the floor. Is there anyone with a mop who can take care of it?" He smiled a dazzling smile.

He hadn't even dropped it before she had the phone in her hand.

"I'll get it sorted right away."

Oh, Jesus.

"Come on. Before she starts giggling," I muttered under my breath.

Luckily, she didn't hear me.

But Jacob Creed did. He gave a low chuckle as he followed me through the hotel to the back room where my office was. I unlocked the door, then flicked on the light as I walked in.

"Can you shut the door behind you? Thanks. Everyone comes in otherwise." I put the order books on my desk next to my computer and clasped my hands together.

Boy, now what did I say?

Hi, how was your weekend? I'm sorry you know what my boobs look like beneath my blouse, Mr. Boss, sir?

"Let's try the introduction thing again." He took a step forward. "Jacob Creed. New owner and, as they tell me, the person in charge."

I hesitated only a second before putting my hand into his much larger one. "Mellie Rogers. Manager and apparent hot mess."

His grip was firm, but it was his smile that once again, captured my attention.

He had the most real kind of smile. Not forced, and you could see it in his eyes, whether it was a smirk or a wide grin like the one he was wearing right now.

It was dangerous.

Daring.

Like crack for my libido, if I was honest.

A knock on the door made me step back and withdraw my hand. "Yes?"

It opened a crack. "I have your ice pack." Brittany's voice came through the gap.

"Oh! Thanks. Come in."

She stepped inside and with her blonde-haired head down, passed me the ice pack.

"Thanks so much. Brittany, this is Jacob Creed, the new owner. Mr. Creed, this is Brittany. She works both reception and concierge."

"Pleasure." He smiled and offered her his hand.

She shook, mumbled something, and excused herself.

Jacob watched her go. "She works with people?"

Despite the pain in my head, I laughed. "You wouldn't think it. She's the shyest person I know, but when she's on concierge, she can find you anything. It's quite remarkable. We should sit down."

"You should put that ice pack on your head." He gave me another pointed look.

With the petulance of a sulky teen, I stared back at him and touched the towel-wrapped pack to the back of my head.

"There we go. I have to admit, it's been a long time since an owner has been here telling me what to do."

He grinned, resting his right ankle on his left knee. He sat right back and, linking his fingers, rested his clasped hands on his lap. "I was told by the previous owner he didn't do much more than invest."

"He hasn't invested in this place in two years." I could barely help the bitterness that crept into my tone. "Isn't it painfully obvious?"

Jacob nodded. "But I knew that when I bought it. Admittedly, it was from photos that seemed to be a little old."

"You bought it without seeing it?"

Another nod. "I'm not from here."

"No. I couldn't tell. You sound so Southern," I drawled.

Another smile from him. "My grandfather recently passed, and the deal on my inheritance was that I had to invest it in a business."

"First, I'm sorry," I said. "Second, and you picked this one?"

He laughed lightly, a deep sound that made the hair on my arms stand on end. "New Orleans fascinates me. I wanted a challenge. Apparently, I found one."

That sounded like it had more than one meaning.

"Well." I switched arms holding my ice pack. "I've worked here since I left school, so anything you want to know, I can tell you. You just gotta ask."

"I'm afraid I have a lot of questions."

"Go ahead." I pulled the ice pack off my head and stretched my arms. That was harder to hold in place than I'd thought.

"It's not about the hotel," he warned me.

"It's fine. If you can't tell, I was born here and never bothered to leave."

A smile formed on those plump lips, and he caught my gaze with his gray one. "Is it normal to have seen more breasts in one weekend than I have in my entire life?"

I opened my mouth to answer it, then froze. My cheeks burned red hot, and I cleared my throat three times before I was able to form any kind of sentence.

"During Mardi Gras, absolutely. It's somewhat of a thing..." I paused again as his smile widened. "And not one I've ever participated in until the hussies who call themselves my best friends made me. So...I'm sorry that you've seen way more of me than you ever should have." Another pause. "And there's something I never thought I'd say."

Jacob burst out laughing. He threw his head back, resting on the top of the crushed velvet chair I hated so much, and just laughed at me. All that did was cause me to blush again, somehow even harder.

Was it too soon to look for a new job? There was no way I could work with him.

I'd embarrassed myself enough times already.

"Believe it or not, I'm not holding that against you." His lips quirked up, eyes flashing with amusement. "I'd seen much worse in much brighter conditions that night."

I coughed. Yep. I needed a new job, didn't I?

"Um, well, you're welcome?" Why did that have to come out as a question? Why did I even say that? Man, I was an idiot. "So, moving on...Let's forget that ever happened and our first meeting was today, shall we?"

"Mellie—can I call you Mellie?" He paused.

I nodded.

Jacob swung his foot onto the floor and sat up, leaning forward to rest his forearm on my desk. His intense gaze held all the possible shades of amusement, and something fluttered in the pit of my belly. "Mellie," he said in a low voice. "Today's meeting wasn't exactly better, was it?"

I swallowed. My tongue slipped out and traced over my lower lip, and even as my cheeks heated, I managed to clear my throat. "Yes, well, I was expecting you here. In my office."

His half-smile never wavered. "We got here eventually."

There was that fluttering again.

I coughed, sliding my chair away from my desk. I stood up beanpole straight and smoothed out my skirt. "Why don't I show you around and introduce you to everyone?"

"That sounds perfect."

UPSIDE #4: YOUR SINGLE FRIENDS ARE SYMPATHETIC TO YOUR PLIGHTS. UNLESS IT'S ALL THEIR FAULT. THEN THEY DON'T GIVE A FUCK.

"I'm going to kill you." I glanced at my phone and almost cut my finger instead of the onion. "Both of you. I'm going to kill you slowly and painfully and I'm going to enjoy every last darn second of it!"

Chloe's eyes widened in her little box on the screen.

Peyton leaned forward. "It's not our fault!"

"You're the ones who made me flash!"

"Technically," Chloe started, "you pulled up your shirt."

"You're not blaming me! I'm the victim here!" I scooped up the diced onion and shoved it into the pot with the ground beef. "You're the ones who told me I'd never see those guys again. Oh, maybe you won't, but I have to see one of them every single day!"

"Maybe he'll be like your old boss," Peyton tried. "Not there."

"Nope. He'll be there all the time. There's no escaping it, you lying hussies. He said as much today. He plans to be as involved as possible."

"Oooh." Chloe swept her hair into a messy bun. "Sounds like he's gonna be steppin' on your toes."

I dropped the knife onto the solid wooden board I was dicing garlic on and glared at the camera. Not even the screen—the camera. "I'd rather he stepped on my toes than saw my boobs!"

"It is pretty awkward," Peyton agreed. "And the whole gin thing? Ouch, Mel. Are you sure you can hang onto your adult card?"

"I'm going to trade it in for a mugshot if we stay friends," I muttered.

"Pish." She waved her hand. "We've been friends our entire lives. You talk so much shit."

"You talking shit is why I'm in this position. Where my boss knows what my boobs look like!"

"I mean, on the upside," Chloe said slowly. "You do have great boobs!"

"Yes, Clo, but that's not the point. Her boss doesn't need to know that!" Peyton sighed.

I pointed my knife at the phone. "You. You shut your bitch ass mouth. You don't get to take my side when this is your fault!"

"All right, fine. Did he like your boobs?"

I paused, slowly lowering the knife. "He said he'd seen worse in brighter light. Or something like that."

"See? Not only did he see your boobs, but he likes them. That's a good thing."

"How is that a good thing?" Chloe asked. "The entire point of this conversation is that him seeing her unfairly perky tits is a bad thing, never mind liking what he saw."

"My boobs aren't unfairly perky." I tossed the garlic into the pot and stirred. "Are they?"

Peyton pursed her lips. "Probably perkier than your C-cup should be."

I blinked. "They're hardly spaniels' ears, Peyt, and I'm twenty-seven, not seventy-seven!"

She moved back from the screen, cupped her boobs, and pushed them together. "You know what happens when I take my bra off? I take out someone's eye!"

"Yeah, you have big boobs, we get it." Chloe rolled her eyes—and so would her B-cup if boobs had eyes. Maybe they rolled her nipples.

"We're getting way off track here." I stirred the spaghetti, then set down the wooden spoon. "The point here is that I flashed my boss on Saturday night after y'all made me, then y'all told me I'd never see him again, and that was a lie!"

"If he liked what he saw," Peyton said. "Why don't you just go the whole shebang? Then you've seen each other's genitals and there's no shame. Or do you need a hook-up? I got a great submission earlier from this guy with a nice thick cock and—"

"Oh look, my spaghetti is done. Bye!" I hung up before she could go any further down her latest attempt at getting me laid and took a deep breath.

My spaghetti was nowhere near done.

But thank the baby Jesus on a unicorn ride that conversation was.

I stared at myself in the mirror of the ladies' bathroom at the hotel. I looked perfectly presentable; I knew that. It was the same fitted, three-quarter-length sleeved blouse I wore every day. I was wearing a black pencil skirt that hugged my figure from my waist to my knees, curving over my hips and ass perfectly.

I buttoned the top two pearly white circles that were glinting at me at in the mirror.

I undid the top one.

I'd never cared so much about my cleavage in my life.

How much was too much? That was a question I hadn't asked myself since I was a teenager and living with my parents, and my answer was invariably different to theirs.

I sighed. There was something wrong with me. Jacob Creed already knew what my boobs looked like. A little cleavage wasn't going to make a difference now, was it?

No. No, it was not.

I shook my head and left the bathroom. He'd emailed me to tell me he'd be in after lunch, and it was now officially after lunch. Where was he?

I wandered back to my office and closed the door. I'd already made the mistake of leaving it open once today and had no intentions of doing that again. I'd dealt with everything from an early drunk to a young mom wondering where she could get diapers for her two-year-old.

Spoiler alert: not in my hotel.

I took a sip from my Berry Refresher and leaned back in my chair. I wanted to kick off my heels but knowing my luck, Jacob would show up just that second.

Three light knocks sounded at my door.

Talk of the devil and all that…

"Who is it?" I called.

"It's Jacob," he replied.

I tucked my hair behind my ear and said, "Come in!"

The door creaked as he pushed it open and joined me. He looked dapper in a light blue shirt with navy slacks and dark brown shoes. His hair was the same wavy style it always was, and he smiled when our eyes met. "Good afternoon. How are you today?"

I returned his smile, steadily ignoring the fluttering in my stomach. "Hi. I'm good. How are you?"

"Perfect. How's everything going today?"

"Well," I said, "I haven't smashed any gin today, so it's already an improvement on yesterday."

Jacob chuckled and took a seat in that stupid crushed velvet chair. He wiggled, adjusting his seating position a few times until he was comfortable. "Has anyone ever told you this is, quite possibly, the most uncomfortable seat in existence?"

Grimacing, I nodded. "Only everyone who's ever been unfortunate enough to sit in it."

"Awesome. That'll be the first thing to be replaced. I'm not stealing your chair, and there's no way I'm working sitting in this damn thing."

I blinked at him, holding my cup halfway up to my mouth. "Why would you be sitting in that chair?"

He raised one dark eyebrow, amusement in his eyes. "There's only one office, and you're in it. I need to be here to oversee renovations when they start, and I can't set up in the lobby now, can I?"

More blinking from me. "Can I set up in the lobby?"

Jacob laughed. "If you must, but I can't see how that would be helpful for you to do your work."

"I've never shared my office. I don't know how to share my office." Damn it. I sounded like a teenager who's just been told they had to share their bedroom with their younger sibling.

Luckily for me, Jacob was still laughing. "I promise I won't get in your way. You won't even know I'm here."

All right, this man clearly didn't own a mirror. There was no way I'd be able to ignore him. I mean, if he were in an art museum, he'd be the Mona Lisa of the place.

He'd also be the resident radiator because he was so fucking hot.

"Um, okay?" I was uncertain. "Don't you think it'll be awkward? I mean, we'll be basically on top of each other. This office isn't that big. I don't even think we could get another desk in here."

I looked around dubiously. No. You couldn't. Between the shelves and my desk and the filing cabinets, there was simply no space.

He clicked his tongue and did the same, his gray eyes scanning the space with the same question I'd just asked myself. Then, slowly, his attention fell on my desk, and a tiny smile teased the corners of his mouth.

I held up my finger and shook my head. "No. No. That would be a disaster." Not to mention, I was the messiest person I knew. I couldn't keep things in line if I'd tried. "Don't even think about it."

"Aw, come on. Would it really be that bad to share an office with me?"

"You're not just proposing sharing an office, Mr. Creed. You're proposing we share a desk, and that's another thing entirely."

"Jake."

"What?"

"My name. Call me Jake."

"But... I can't."

He raised his eyebrows. "Why not?"

I swallowed. "You're my boss."

He stood up, grinning, and walked to the window where he leaned against the sill. "And your boss is telling you to call him Jake."

He had me there.

"Fine, *Jake*. But I still don't see how us sharing an office will be anything less than awkward."

"I don't see it being awkward at all. I promise not to sit across from you and picture you topless."

My cheeks burned, but he just grinned.

"Look, try it. If it's super awkward, we'll figure something else out, but I really need a base here at the hotel."

I was going to regret this. I knew it. He might not sit and think about me topless, but I already knew it'd sure as hell be easy to picture him naked about ten times a day.

Sweet Jesus, I was screwed.

"Okay, but my desk is a hot mess," I tried. It was my last attempt at getting him to give up on this idea. "There's stuff everywhere."

"So, tidy it."

I blinked at him. "It's all organized."

"You just said it was a hot mess."

"It's an organized hot mess."

"There's no such thing as an organized hot mess, Mellie."

I held out my hands. "I show up for work every day on time looking like a human being. I beg to differ."

Jake stopped. His gazed danced slowly over my face before his flat expression brightened with the upturn of his lips and the silent laughter that make his eyes shine almost hypnotically. "Touché," he muttered. "But, it still needs tidying. Organized mess or not, I can't work in that."

"I don't have the time to organize it. I have to do the roster."

He leaned forward, flattening his hands on top of two folders. His upper arms tensed, and the sun coming in through the open window played against the dips and curves of the muscles his short sleeves allowed me to see.

Man. You could bounce a quarter off those biceps.

It'd probably bounce so hard it'd take out a window— or an eye—but it'd be worth it.

"I can't decide," he said in a low voice, his expression still amused, but somehow…darker. "If you're trying to be a child about this, or if that's just how things are going to be. Because if it's the latter, this isn't going to work."

I was being a child. Whatever.

I folded my arms and leaned back in my chair. One of my eyebrows raised in a perfect arch, and I met his eyes without flinching. "You might be the new owner and my new boss, *Mr. Creed*, but that doesn't give you the right to tell me you're sharing my office and now, apparently, my desk. It allows you open a discussion about it."

"Is that right?"

"I'm not in the habit of lying." I stood, letting my hands fall to the side. I wasn't going to look up at him anymore, and it worked because he lifted his head to keep hold of my gaze, even if he didn't straighten his back. "I don't like the idea of you sharing my office. I'm not going to change my mind, and I'm not going to pretend I do. If that means I glare at you ten times an hour, you'll have to deal with it."

"I'll have to deal with it?"

Was I making him angrier or more amused? I couldn't tell.

"Yes. Because you're the one who forced yourself in here without considering if it might be even remotely awkward and uncomfortable or if you might encroach on my own work."

He was stony-faced. No emotion whatsoever peered back at me. Not from his mouth, not his jaw, and not his eyes. He was like a robot, but I knew his brain was whirring. His gaze was too solid and intense, despite being almost cold in its vacant-like stare.

"I don't know if your attitude is amusing to me or if I can't stand it."

Well, that feeling was borderline mutual.

"If you can't stand it, let me know. I know where the door is. I've walked through it enough times in the last nine years. More times than any owner of this place has." I picked up my drink, sipped it quickly, and set it back down. "Now, if you don't mind, if we're done, I have to track down who's requesting what hours."

I walked around my desk and past him, heading for the door. Only, before I could get there, his arm shot out, his fingers wrapping around my wrist and stopping me in my tracks. I wobbled on my heels but managed to keep my balance as I turned to glare at him.

Jake stepped forward, almost threateningly close to me. "You won't walk out, Mellie. I don't have to be here forever to know you love this job. You'd only leave if you were forced to."

"You sound awfully like you're considering it anyway," I bit out.

Slowly, a half-smile tugged at his lips. "No. Just thinking out loud. And again—my name is Jake, not Mr. Creed."

"I don't care."

"I do. Call me it again, and I have half a mind to throw you over my knee."

My jaw dropped. Did he just—no! "I'm not a child, Mr. Creed. I don't need you to spank me."

Why did I say that out loud?

"You might not need me to, but you'd sure as hell want me to carry on once I started."

I yanked my wrist from his grip, and steadfastly ignoring that stupid, sexy grin on his face, turned and stalked out of the room before I could say something I'd regret.

Knowing my luck, I'd end up pulling my skirt up for him.

This was a bad, bad idea.

UPSIDE #5: WHENEVER YOU ASK IF YOUR BUTT LOOKS BIG IN THIS, YOU KNOW YOU'LL GET THE TRUTH FROM THE MIRROR.

I licked the last of the sugar from my fingers and threw the donut box into the trash. Wednesdays were my favorite days. I didn't have to work until two, which meant I could lie in bed until nine and eat donuts for breakfast without wearing pants.

Sure, this morning I was wearing shorts, but that was because I'd had to see the mailman, and I didn't think he wanted to see my underpants.

I wandered over to my coffee machine right as my phone rang. The shrill noise filled the area of the small room, and I almost jumped as I scrambled across to the microwave to grab it from the top.

"Hello?" I answered, turning around and—a searing pain shot through my big toe. "Owww, motherfucker! Ow, ow, ow!" I grabbed my foot, which left me hopping, and ultimately, I almost fell against the cabinet. "I'll call you back!" I shouted at whoever the hell had called me and hung up.

I gripped my toe tightly, biting the inside of my cheek. Man, there was nothing worse than stubbing your toe. It throbbed like hell, a dead, dull ache that reminded me of the time I broke my second toe.

No. I couldn't break another toe. That was the worst thing ever.

I squeezed my eyes shut and counted to ten through the pain. Thankfully, by the time I reached ten, the pain was slowly ebbing from "cut it off!" to "can I have a cuddle?" on the pain scale.

Knock. Knock. Knock.

I glared at my front door as if it had knocked itself. Gingerly, I set my foot back down and awkwardly limped toward the door. Squinting so I could see through the peephole, I froze.

What the fucking hell was he doing here?

Forgetting about my toe, I yanked open my front door and stared at my boss. "What the hell are you doing here?"

"Well," he said, holding out a phone. "I called you, and right after you answered, you started screaming. Given that I'm already familiar with your clumsiness, I thought I'd check on you."

"How did you—what? Are you my neighbor or something? That was two minutes ago!"

"No. I was outside."

"Why in God's name were you outside my house?"

He grinned. "I was hoping I could steal a few hours of your time. But now, I'm hoping you didn't almost kill yourself."

Lame. I was so lame. And so dramatic.

"I stubbed my toe," I muttered. "Forgot the table was there."

"That must have been quite the stub," Jake said, fighting a smile. "Now, can I come in, or are you going to show the entire neighborhood your nipples?"

I jerked, dropping my head down and, yes. I was going to show the entire neighborhood my nipples. I wasn't wearing a bra, and they were apparently trying to stage an escape through the front of my shirt.

Great.

Just. Freaking. Great.

Why couldn't I keep my boobs under wraps around this guy?

I clamped my arm over my chest and spun on the balls of my feet. He laughed and followed me inside. At least, I think he did. I practically ran to the stairs and up them to my room.

Note to self: start sleeping in a bra if it means keeping these boobs in line.

I rifled through my doors but came up empty. There were no bras. How could there be no bras? I had about ten, not that anyone would believe me if I said so. They had to all be in the laundry.

I crept back downstairs and through to the laundry room. They were all either dirty or wet. Where was the one I wore yesterday? That was still clean. I'd worn it once, and taken it off—

Oh no.

I'd come home, and before I'd eaten my dinner, I'd grabbed a tank top and whipped off my bra…

In my living room.

Where I presumed, Jake was right now.

This…Well, this was just going from bad to worse and back again.

Clutching one arm over my chest again, I shuffled into the front room.

"Looking for something?" he asked, reclined on my sofa with his nose in the middle of Cosmo.

"Um, yes. I left something in here." Where was it? Where was it? Come on, eyes. Look faster!

Without removing his attention from the magazine, he pointed to the floor next to him. "Your bra is right here on top of the clothes you wore yesterday."

Of course. Of course, it was. Why the hell wouldn't it be?

I coughed to hide the fact I wanted to choke to death with embarrassment and grabbed the clothes. Jake glanced to the side and met my eye, his lips curved but twitching like he was doing everything possible not to burst out laughing.

I quickly turned and darted away.

And banged my shin on the coffee table.

I gave a sharp intake of breath, but I didn't stop running.

Because the bastard was laughing. *Hard.* And if I stopped, I'd punch him while I cried.

I ran upstairs and threw myself on the bed. "Fuck, hell, shit, ass, ahhh!" I rolled while grabbing my shin, then relaxed, huffing out a huge breath.

I had to shut the door to drown out the new round of laughter from Jake.

Of all the people in the world who could buy the hotel…

I shook that thought off. At least I'd showered this morning, so all I had to do was run the brush back through my hair.

I dressed, triple checking to make sure I had my bra on, then went back downstairs to face the music.

The floorboards creaked as I made it to the open-plan downstairs. Jake peeked over the top of the magazine. He'd made himself comfortable. Shoes off, feet up, cushions rearranged.

"Comfy?" I asked.

He nodded, dropping the magazine to his lap. "I thought I should, given that everything happens in threes. Good for you for getting dressed without hurting yourself again!"

I tugged up the waistband of my jeans and glared at him. "It is not funny."

"It really is. Now I understand why you call yourself an organized hot mess." He grinned.

"If I were organized, I'd have had a clean bra in my bedroom," I muttered. "What are you doing here? Wait—how do you even know where I live?"

He sat up, setting the magazine back on my coffee table. "I'm your boss. I have all the employee records."

"It's my morning off." There was no use telling him those weren't for personal use. I doubted he'd pay attention. "Why are you here?"

"I need furniture for your—our—office. Better desktop storage for your chaos so I don't want to throw myself off the room, and a better chair for me so I don't throw *it* off the fucking roof."

I snorted. "And why do you need me for that?"

He put his shoes back on and, leaning forward, rested his elbows on his knees. I'd been too busy avoiding looking at him that I hadn't noticed how nicely that white polo shirt hugged his broad shoulders. The light tan he sported made the shirt even whiter. And he was wearing jeans!

"Because," he smiled, "It's your office, so you can choose it all. Except for the chair. If your ass isn't gonna sit on it, you don't get to choose it."

"So, technically, I'm working."

He paused. "No. You're…helping."

"Nope. I'm working. If I'm with my boss and I'm buying things for my place of work, I'm working." I leaned against the edge of my desk and folded my arms.

Jake sighed, stood, and walked toward me, grabbing something from the table. "Has anyone ever told you you're absolutely impossible?"

"I was a teenage girl once. Of course, they have. It was my middle name at one point." I had to peer up to meet his eyes when he'd stopped right in front of me. "It's my morning off. I don't have to come with you to do this."

His lips twisted into a wry smile. "Fine. I'll pay you overtime."

I flattened my hand against my chest and, with my best innocent look, said, "You will? That's so sweet?"

"Right. Sweet." He handed me a Berry Refresher. I'd been too busy looking at his eyes to notice it. "Here. To wake you up."

"How did you—never mind. Thank you." Damn it, now I was smiling at it.

"Grab your stuff. Let's go. We need to make a stop first." He headed for the door.

I snatched up my things and threw them in my favorite purse. "Where?"

"The UPS store."

"Why?"

He pulled open the door and looked at me, smirking. "To buy you bubble wrap before you hurt yourself again."

"If you weren't my boss, I'd punch you for that."

"And you'd probably end up hurting yourself more."

"Shut up."

Thankfully, I managed to convince Jake that the ups store wasn't necessary because I was, in fact, an adult. In was also perfectly capable of not breaking ten bones in a day... at least, that was the story I was sticking to.

I couldn't promise I wouldn't break his though.

One hour. We'd been looking at chairs for an hour. I almost wanted to call every ex I'd ever had and apologize for all the times I'd taken them shopping and they'd wanted to kill me.

Then again, clothing shopping was a very serious business. Office chair buying? Not so much.

"For the love of God, Jake. It's a chair. Anyone would think you're a princess trying to avoid a non-existent pea!"

He spun around once in a black, leather, high-backed computer chair. "I need the right chair. It's not as simple as walking in and just buying something."

"Hello, I'm a woman. I'm an expert at shopping. Pleased to meet you."

"This isn't a pair of shoes. This is an important work chair."

"Have you seen the price of Louboutins?"

Jake paused. "I can't say I've ever imagined myself in four-inch-heels, actually."

I stared at him. "Pick. A. Chair. We haven't even touched upon the office section yet, and I have to get to work soon."

"I can say your boss won't mind if you're late because of this."

"He might not, but there are almost one hundred employees who will wonder where the hell their manager is."

He tapped a finger against his chin. "Here. What do you think of this chair?"

"Seriously? That's your response to what I said? Christ on a cracker."

"I'm not sure why you'd want to put Jesus on a cracker, but yes, seriously."

I eyed him with annoyance as he stood, motioning for me to take a seat. I did it, shuffling along the floor, never letting my eyes leave him. His smile grew with every step I took, and finally, reluctantly, I stopped in front of the chair and lowered myself down.

Soft.

Like a cloud.

A cloud covered with cold, soft leather.

"Ohhh." I leaned back, closing my eyes. "I think I just came a little."

Jake barked out a laugh.

Shit.

I said that out loud.

I snapped my eyes open. "I mean—shit."

"Two of those, then," he said, composing himself.

"I don't—there's nothing wrong with my chair now." I jumped out of the chair like my ass was on fire. "Shall we go to the office section?"

He stared at me for a moment, but he didn't say anything. He wanted to—it was written all over his face. In the glint of his eyes and the barely-there twitch of his lips. In the stretch of his jaw and the scratch of his chin.

Those things told me I didn't want to hear what he didn't say.

Why did my boss have to be hot? And know what my boobs looked like?

Man, would I ever get past that?

No.

No, I would not.

"Let's go," Jake said after that everlasting moment of eye-glinting and chin-scratching.

Was it bad that I wanted to scratch his chin for him? I bet that stubble could tickle a girl's fingertips just right.

Sweet Jesus! I was *this close* to goddamn therapy.

"Mellie? Are you coming?"

"Am I wha—" I stopped and, not seeing him, flailed as I spun around. "Yes. I am."

"You're in a little world of your own, aren't you?" The smile on his face was unmoving.

Did he ever not smile?

"Well, I didn't stub my toe and break my shin by being on this planet, did I?" I shot him a look as I swept past him to the escalator to go upstairs.

Jake took the step immediately behind me. "What time are you supposed to start?"

"Two o'clock. Why?"

"We need to move." He prodded my back.

"Why? What time is it?" I jerked around to look at him.

"One-fifteen."

"Jake!"

"Top of the escalator!"

"What?" I turned a second too late and tripped over the tiny step that led from the escalator to the still floor.

Luckily for me, Jake was close enough to me that he was able to grab me and steady me, stopping me from falling flat on my face.

"Oh my God," I breathed.

Putting both his hands on my upper arms, he dragged me out of the way of the escalator and looked right into my eyes. "I knew we should have stopped at UPS."

UPSIDE #6: YOU CAN CONVINCE THE PIZZA GUY THAT SIXTEEN-INCH PIZZA IS TO SHARE WITH YOUR "BOYFRIEND." EXCEPT YOU GET TO EAT IT ALL.

I barely made it to work on time, and that was only thanks to the taxi I'd called to get me out of that store. One thing was for sure: if a man ever complained about my shopping again, I'd direct him to Jacob Creed.

Even I never wanted to see the inside of a mall again.

I rifled through the paperwork on my desk. There were sticky notes and message cards all over the place. Disregarding half of the messages, I pushed them to the side and picked up one of the messages from the maids.

"Nope," I said instantly and threw it in the trash. There were certain times of the month you could request vacations. The day after I put up the rosters was not that time.

I moved quickly through the rest of them, splitting them between important and…well, a load of shit. As usual, there was more crap than anything else, including a cold caller from a plumber who claimed to have started servicing our boiler.

Nope.

Man, today was full of nope.

Stubbing my toe? Nope. Being braless? Nope. Jake showing up and forcing me into the most hellish shopping trip of my life? Nope.

Big. Fat. Nope.

I sighed and leaned back in my chair. Damn it. I should have taken Jake up on the offer of a new chair. After sitting in that sigh-worthy one, I felt like I needed it. And like this one felt like sitting on a rock.

Double sigh…

I picked up the message from the person who I needed to call back.

I didn't really want to have the conversation right now, but it was better than sitting here doing nothing.

I dialed the number and listened.

Ring, ring, ring.

The call rolled over to voicemail. I returned the message and hung up. Then, I sighed. Again. There was a lot of that going around today.

I was seconds away from lamenting the terrible mess of this day when the door opened with a loud creak.

In keeping with classic Mellie, I screamed.

Jake jumped about ten feet back into the hallway. I clasped my hand to my chest and glared at him.

"What the hell?" My voice was louder than I'd intended it to be, but he'd scared the shit out of me!

"What do you mean, "what the hell?"" Jake asked, stepping inside. "You're the one who's in here screaming like I'm a ghost coming to kill you."

I slapped my hand on the table. "You may as well be," I said. "Haven't you heard of knocking?"

Jake closed the door behind him "Yeah, well, I didn't think I had to knock to get into my own office."

"Well, you thought wrong," I said, standing and waving my finger at him. "Because this is our office, not yours. *Ours.*"

He raised one eyebrow in amusement. "Are you going to knock before you come in here?"

"No, why would I?"

He chuckled. "Because, as you just insisted, this is our office, not my office." Shrugging off his jacket, he finished, "Which means it's not *your* office either."

I blinked at him. "That might be right, but technically speaking, it is my office."

"Well, make up your mind." He smirked. "Because it can't be your office and our office at the same time."

"Fine, it's my office." I crossed my arms over my chest. "is that better? You know as well as I do you're like, like, like… an office thief."

"An office thief."

Damn it; he was laughing at me again. I could see in his eyes. I was really starting to hate it when he did that.

I rose my chin in defiance. "Yes. An office thief." I nodded my head once, strongly, as if to prove my point.

I didn't know what my point was, but still, I felt I had to make it.

That was how it worked, right?

Jake walked over to the window and looked outside. "An office thief," he muttered, seemingly to himself. "I've been called many things, but that's a new one."

"I could come up with a few more if you really wanted me to."

"No, I think I'm good, thanks. God only knows what you come up with after that shopping trip."

"Ah, see you admit it was like entering the seventh ring of hell for you too, huh?"

He paused, eyes twinkling. "No... Not exactly..."

Man, this would be really awkward if I cared."

his laughter echoed through the office. "Don't worry, Mellie. That was pretty obvious you wanted to kill me."

I touched my hand to my chest and sighed in a mock relief. "Oh, thank God, I'm so glad. On the other hand," I paused. "If your body is ever found, I'll be the first suspect. Never mind. Forget I said anything. Shopping isn't worth killing somebody over."

Jake snorted. "Clearly, you've never watched forensic files."

"No," I said slowly, "And after that shopping trip, you should be glad I haven't."

He held my gaze for a moment and then burst out laughing.

What was it about that laugh?

It was like... Magic. Every time I'd heard it, it'd given me goosebumps. And I'd heard it a lot lately. It never seemed to get old.

You know what was getting old?

The way those stupid ass goosebumps danced up and down my arms every single time I heard it.

Oh, and look, there they were again, the little traitors.

I didn't want to feel them. Actually, as a point of note, I didn't want to hear him laugh either.

"Fair enough," Jake said. "In that case, definitely don't watch it. It's terrible."

I sat back down the narrowed my eyes at him. He had a stupid grin on his face – one that reached his eyes and made them shine.

I was really, really starting to hate that one as well. And that was all the tummy butterflies' faults.

Again: why couldn't I have an ugly boss?

"No, actually, I think I *will* check it out. Just in case. Sounds educational." Then, as he stared at me as if he was trying to decide whether or not to laugh, I let my own grin take over my face.

"Okay, fine." He came over to the desk and sat down on the velvet chair. "But if you hate it, don't blame me when you've wasted three hours of your life planning how to murder somebody in five different ways."

"I don't know, that sounds like some pretty valuable information…"

"On one hand, it is. But, on the other, they already know how to solve the crime because they've done it once before."

Once again, I narrowed my eyes. "Now, see, I don't know if you're just saying that, or if you're really looking up from my well-being here."

He feigned a gasp. "Would I do anything but?"

"I don't know." I leaned back in my chair and tapped my pen against the table. "Would you?" I punctuated the question with one raise of my eyebrows and a half-grin.

"Hey, you." He leaned forward and pointed a finger at me, his smile shining in those wild, gray eyes. "I found your bra this morning. That is definitely looking out for your well-being, especially after the greeting I got when I showed up at your house."

"Okay, mister." Now, it was my turn to wave my finger. Or, rather, a pen. My bright pink highlighter waved in circles in front of his face as I stood and leaned over the table to make my point. "If we're going to share an office, which I'm still against, by the way, then we are going to have to set some ground rules to be able to work together successfully."

"I feel like you're about to pull out a whiteboard and write them all down so I remember them."

"Don't you…" I stilled the pen and, with annoyance, yanked a pad of plain paper out from my drawer. With a little too much vigor, I opened the pad then slapped it down on my desk. "Yes, let's do that. And, if you want, I'll even go to reception and have photocopied a few times in case you happen to lose the original."

Grinning, he said, "Could you get any more sarcasm in that last sentence?"

"Yes, actually, I could. Don't test me. You might be surprised." Or offended. That was known to happen.

Really, in the twenty-first century, you'd think everyone would get sarcasm. Nope.

"Damn, that sounds like a challenge."

"Shut up and stop trying to distract me." I uncapped the pen with a pop. "Right. Rule one."

"I think I know where this is going." He ran his fingers through his hair, his lips twitching into a smile the entire time.

Usually, I wanted to lick that smile. But now? No, no. Now, I kind of wanted to slap it off his face.

Yep. We needed some ground rules. He needed to stop talking about my boobs, and I needed to stop wanting to either, a: kiss him or, b: hit him.

I scrawled "rule one" onto the pad. "Rule one. Do. Not. Talk. About. Mellie's. Boobs." I underlined it several times to get my point across. "Is that clear?"

Jake leaned over the desk and looked at the pad. "Your handwriting is kinda messy there, so no, not clear at all."

I threw the pen onto the desk. It hit nib-first, leaving a bright pink dot on the pad before it fell over and rolled onto the floor. "And you tell me I'm impossible?"

His grin was playful—boyish, almost, and it reached right up to his eyes. "I just don't get why you're making such a big deal out of this. It's only awkward because you're making it awkward."

"You keep mentioning my boobs."

"It's hard not to when you answer your door without a bra, only for that bra to be on the floor."

"You didn't even need to be at my house. It's totally your fault."

Jake rolled his eyes and sat back again. "Let it go, Mellie. The sooner you accept that I'm your boss and me knowing what your boobs look like doesn't bother me, the easier this will be."

I blinked at him. "It doesn't bother you?"

"I'm not saying my inner teenage boy doesn't flash back sometimes, but…"

"Ugh!" I clamped my arms firmly over my chest. Not that it would help the thoughts inside his head, mind you, but still. I felt better. "This is why it bothers me."

"If it bothers you, maybe you shouldn't have listened to your friends in the first place."

"They told me I'd never see you again," I muttered.

"Well, that plan is going fucking spectacularly, don't you think?"

"Are you allowed to cuss at work?"

"I'm the boss. I can do what I want at work."

"Oy." Now, I was the one rolling my eyes. "Look, let's just not mention my boobs, and then I'll be able to move on. Eventually. I hope."

He studied me, gaze dropping to my chest for a moment. "No, you won't. You'll still blush every time our eyes meet."

"I do not blush every time."

One dark eyebrow quirked in amusement. "You sure do. Just like you are now."

"I'm not blushing," I lied, holding his gaze steady.

"You really, really are."

Ugh!

I stood up and pointed at him. "I don't have to take this."

"Take what? That I'm right and you're wrong?" Laughter. It danced in his eyes once again.

"No. Just...This!" Dramatically waving my arms around in a flailing fashion, I stomped once, then headed toward the door. "If you need me, tough. I'm going to find something to manage."

"That is your job!" he shouted after me, laughing.

Oooh. I was really starting to hate him.

UPSIDE #7: YOU NEVER HAVE TO DEAL WITH MAN FLU. JUST MENSTRUATION, BUT THAT'S A LICENSE TO WHINE.

Me: *I'm not coming into work today. I'm sick.*

I left the lying text screen open on my phone and headed to my bathroom for a shower. I wasn't sick. I was sick of the situation I was in and it'd only been a few days. Why couldn't I get over it?

Oh, because Jacob Creed was my boss. Not only was he my boss, but he was handsome and, to my annoyance, disarmingly charming. His laugh gave me goosebumps and his smile started off a whole pack of butterflies in my stomach.

It was a schoolgirl crush, based upon nothing but the way he looked.

It was ridiculous, and I needed to talk myself out of this stupid crush. Except the only thing I'd ever successfully talked myself out of was a diet.

I wasn't exactly the poster girl for self-control.

I lathered my hair with shampoo.

I was a wimp. A bonafide pussy. Why was I acting like I was thirteen instead of handling this situation like the grown woman I was?

I rinsed the shampoo.

I could handle this. I didn't need to be sick. I could make a miraculous recovery or use today to form a game plan. Maybe there was an answer on Google. Surely, somewhere, the in depths of the interwebs, there was a person who'd written on some obscure forum to get information about what to do when one's boss has seen one's boobs.

I turned off the shower and wrapped myself in a towel before twisting my hair into another one. My phone was flashing with a new text message when I walked back into my room, so I picked it up to see how successful my attempt at calling off work was.

Jake: *Embarrassment isn't an illness.*

Darn it.

Me: *I happen to have it chronically.*
Jake: *I happened to have an inappropriate dream last night, but I'm not calling off work just so I don't have to face you.*

My jaw dropped.
So did my phone.
Was he—was he serious?
Another message came through.

Jake: *Get your ass to work. And are those skirts in the dress code?*
Me: *I am not having this conversation!!!! This is not okay!!!!!*
Jake: *The dream thing or the skirts thing?*
Me: *WHY IS THIS EVEN A QUESTION????*

My phone rang, his name flashing on the screen, and I answered it, only to shout, "I'm not talking to you!"

"Well, then, hello, whoever it is answering the phone. Can you pass me to Mellie?"

"This is inappropriate. I'm not having this conversation with you. I'm sick. I'm walking away from the phone now." I fake-coughed twice.

I knew watching *Mean Girls* would help me fake-cough one day.

"Are the skirts a uniform code?" he went on, completely ignoring me.

I didn't respond.

"You're blushing right now, aren't you?"

Still, didn't say anything.

"All right, they're a dress code. I won't complain about it."

Still silent.

"Mellie, you can pretend you aren't on the phone, but I can hear you breathing. Either you're holding it, or you're busy."

"Goodbye!" I shouted, hanging up.

I threw the phone on my bed. Almost instantly, the screen lit up with a new message.

Jake. Again.

Against my better judgment, I picked up the phone.

Jake: *Messing with you. No inappropriate dreams.*

Jake: *Get your ass to work. Embarrassment doesn't excuse you when you're the cause of your own.*

Me: *If you weren't my boss...*

Jake: *You'd flash me more than your boobs?*

Me: *You do NOT want to know what I want to say to you right now.*

Jake: *I'll take that as a no.*

———— ⌐•◦•⌐ ————

I dumped my purse on the desk with a sigh. Jake was clearly already here because all of my things had been helpfully put into two boxes and set near my computer. He'd even taped a note to the computer screen that told me the new stuff was being delivered today so I had to tidy my mess.

It would have been a lot easier to tidy if he'd left me to do it. It was an organized mess. I could find everything. Now? God knows where it all was.

I was going to need more coffee to handle this.

I rubbed my hand over my chin, grabbed my keys, and left my office. Stopping only to lock it, I walked through the hotel to the bar and slipped behind it. It was still early, and it wasn't actually open yet, so that meant I could make my coffee in peace.

I hummed to myself as I started the machine and grabbed a mug.

What came out was not fresh coffee.

I stopped it and checked. It hadn't been cleaned.

Now, I was annoyed.

I dropped my unnecessarily dirty mug in the sink beneath the bar and printed some receipt paper from the register. I wrote a quick, annoyed note for someone to clean it and went back to the office to see who had been responsible for it.

Jake was waiting outside the office when I arrived with a scowl on my face. "Wow. Did I do that to your face?"

I glared at him. "Why are you waiting outside?"

"You have the only office key."

I glanced down at the key in my hand. "Oh. I'll get another cut at lunch." I unlocked the door and left him to follow me inside. "And yes, you are partially responsible for my face, as you so kindly put it."

"What happened?"

I pointed to the boxes. "Plus, when I went to get coffee, the machine hadn't been cleaned. It's supposed to be cleaned every night."

His eyebrows went up. "Good thing I stopped at the café on the corner, then."

I finally looked at what he was holding. Two coffee cups and a brown bag. "What's that?"

"Most people call it coffee. I'm calling it…a mixture of an apology and a goodwill gesture."

"You are."

He nodded. "One, for being a slight ass to you this morning."

A slight ass.

"Two, because I think we need to make peace with the awkward side of our relationship. I promise never to bring up your wonderful breasts again."

"The wonderful part doesn't give me much hope."

"What? Can't I even compliment them on the only time I'm allowed to refer to them? Cut a man some slack, woman."

I met his eyes and with a twist of my lips, nodded. "Fine. We're at a truce. I think I can cope with this."

Jake held up one finger and put both the coffee and the bag down. "You definitely will when you see what's inside this bag."

I sniffed. The sweet scent of powdered sugar reached my nose. "Beignets?"

He shook his head.

I wrinkled my face up and then... "Donuts?"

He grinned. Wide. "Donuts."

I reached for the bag like a starving lunatic and dove my hand inside. Instantly, my fingertips connected with the still warm dough. I grabbed and tugged one out, biting into it and sending sugar flying all over the papers stacked in the box in front of me.

I moaned. If there was anything better than sugar donuts, it was warm sugar donuts.

Ninety-nine percent sure they were the way to my heart.

If I ever got proposed to and there weren't donuts, I'd have to seriously consider it.

Jake watched me with a crooked smile as I inhaled the first donut. I was more than aware that I had sugar not only on my desk, but all over myself and my clothing. I didn't care. It was so damn good I didn't have time to pretend I was a civilized human being.

"How did you know I like donuts?" I licked my fingers.

"Like donuts? You look like you're in a committed relationship from that display." He chuckled and sat down. "Your kitchen smelled like them. I took a lucky guess."

He dropped his hand into the bag and pulled one out. I stared at him as he took a bite.

"Relax," he said. "I bought ten."

"Clearly, you aren't aware of just how committed our relationship is." I pulled another out and, this time, grabbed one of the napkins and sat down before tearing into it. "Thank you," I said.

Our eyes met. "You're welcome. Who's responsible for the lack of coffee?"

"Oh!" I'd been distracted by the donuts. I licked my fingers again and pulled the roster file from my cupboard. I flicked through to this week's and ran my nail down the list. "Harley. Of course."

Jake looked at me quizzically, so I filled him in on the mess that was Harley, including the explanation as to why I was on the floor the day he came in.

"Why not fire her?" he asked as if it were the simplest thing in the world.

I sighed. "Because she can mix drinks, and well. She's just not so great at all the other stuff."

"Hmm," was all he said.

I waited for him to elaborate, but when he didn't, I shook it off and finished my donut.

"All right," Jake said, standing up. "I'm going to meet with the builders, and I'll be back after lunch. Do you need anything?"

I paused. "No… I'm good. Thank you."

"I can get the key cut."

"It's fine. My uncle owns a place." I smiled.

"All right, then. I'll see you later." He returned my smile, grabbed his phone, and left.

I took one look at the boxes and picked up another donut.

———⋄◈⋄———

"I just—I don't get it." I threw myself onto the sofa and almost sent the box of donuts flying onto the floor.

Thankfully, Peyton was quicker than the box. She grabbed it and sat back, hugging it to herself. "First, watch the donuts. I got the last two pink sprinkles, and I'm partial to them." She stroked the top of the box. "Second, what don't you get? How doesn't he care about your boobs? I don't care about them either."

"You're not supposed to care about my boobs. You're a woman, for a start."

"I care about your boobs," Chloe interrupted, tucking her blond hair behind her ear. "I think you have great boobs. Bra or no bra."

"Usually no bra," Peyton added.

"I'm not afraid to throw something at you," I warned her. "This is awkward."

"Ugh! Get over yourself, Melanie!" Peyton snapped her fingers. "You are a grown woman. He is a grown man. He saw your tits. So what? Steven Lawrence saw your tits five times in junior year."

I snatched a donut from the box. *Don't tell my hips.* "We were dating! It's entirely different!"

Chloe delicately picked up a white-iced donut before saying, "She's right. It is different, Peyt. They were dating, and Jacob is her boss. You can't expect her to just get over that. It is partly your fault."

"It's just as much your fault," Peyton reminded her, then looked at me and nodded toward Chloe. "Drunky smurf over here shook her Tic-Tacs like she was in front of a bachelor party leaving a curry house."

I choked on my laughter. "That's not the point. You got us drunk. It's almost entirely your fault."

"Look, sunshine," she said, tearing a bite of donut off the ring so her words were muffled. "I didn't grab your shirt and whip it up like a two-dollar hooker on overtime. You did that, so grow a pair and take responsibility for your actions."

"You sound like you don't want to take responsibility for yours."

"Hey. You're big girls. You can refuse cocktails."

Chloe and I shared a glance. "Refuse cocktails?" she said. "I don't understand."

"You have us mixed up with your other friends," I continued. "But, wait. You don't have other friends."

"I have plenty of friends," Peyt said.

"Friends without penises. Or benefits."

She paused. "We're not talking about me. We're talking about your hot boss who knows what your tits look like."

"You're not helping."

"I'm not trying to help. I'm trying to slap your size-eight ass into reality, you idiot."

"Slap mine into reality and I'm putting yours on a catapult. Right into the middle of the Gulf." I tore my donut in two and gave her boobs a pointed look. "I always wondered if silicone would float."

Chloe choked, almost spitting wine across the coffee table.

Peyton gasped, shoving the donut box to the table, then clasping her hands to her chest. "They are not fake, and you know it!"

"So does half the graduating class of our high school!"

"Oookay!" Chloe waved her hands between us. "I have a migraine. Shut your asses."

I sighed. "Migraines and tension headaches are different. Migraines you get randomly. Tension headaches come when you're near Peyton."

"Oooh, you bitch!" Peyton launched a donut at me.

"Hey, hey, hey! Bitching is no reason to be cruel to donuts!" I caught and held the donut to me. "Ooh, and it's a pink sprinkles one."

Her eyes widened. "No. That's mine. Please give it back."

I looked at the donut and then her. "I don't know. I like these, too. It won't talk about my boobs, that's for sure."

Peyt whimpered. "I love your boobs. He's a fool for not loving your boobs. No more ass slapping unless you ask me. Please give back my donut."

"Interesting," Chloe said, stroking an imaginary beard. "The weakness is strong with this one."

"My donut," Peyt whispered.

I held it out, then quickly whipped it away from her when she reached for it. "Tell me what to do with Hot Boss."

"Me?" She pointed toward Chloe. "She's the one who runs the dating website."

"She's also been in love with your brother since before she had a period."

"I can hear that," Chloe muttered. "And I'm not in love with Dom."

Peyton grimaced. "Good point. Is the fate of the donut really resting on the slut of the group's advice?"

"You said that," Chloe added, looking up from the donut box she'd hijacked sometime between the bickering. "So we can just agree. Even if I don't think you're a slut."

"You don't?" I asked, grinning. "It depends on the day for me."

Peyton rolled her eyes, but her lips twitched. "Look, I'm okay with being free. I just saw a video on Facebook of a woman with over a thousand cats. I like cats, but not that much, and I don't want to be that kind of cat lady."

"Where would you keep a thousand pussies?" Chloe frowned.

I didn't even need to think about it. "Pornhub."

Slowly, my two best friends turned to look at me. Then, as if they'd synced it, burst out laughing.

The donuts?

Well, my rug got a makeover.

UPSIDE #8: YOU WON'T FALL DOWN THE TOILET BECAUSE THE SEAT IS UP. UNLESS YOU JUST CLEANED IT. THEN THAT'S A BUTT-FULL OF PEE-WATER.

I squealed as I tipped backward on the porcelain. Instantly, I gripped the sides of the toilet seat and shoved myself off it, clenching my Kegels harder than I ever had in my life in the process.

I did not need to pee down my leg today. No way. Nuh-uh.

"Mother—" I stalled, shutting myself up by grinding my teeth together.

Unfortunately, I was at work, and I did not want any tiny, unsuspecting ears who may or may not have been outside to hear me cussing up a storm.

I put the toilet seat down, dried my butt with tissue, and sat back on the seat.

The best thing about this hotel was the fact it was an old home turned hotel. It was a huge house, once upon a time, and the renovations had been simple. This meant that my office, which was once servants quarters, had a tiny bathroom attached. It was just big enough for a sink and a toilet.

I loved it. It meant I could work until I was about to pee myself—helpful, especially if I was comfortable.

Now, when I say I loved it, I mean, I loved it. As in, did.

Since I was no longer the sole user of the tiny bathroom, it became apparent that not even my pee breaks were sacred.

What kind of fresh hell had I stepped into?

First, he saw my boobs. Now, he left the toilet seat up.

I don't know what I did to piss off karma, but I was over it.

After finishing my business up in the bathroom, I went back into the office. Jake had his head buried in his laptop; chin dipped, eyes down.

I side-eyed him as I walked past him. There was no way he hadn't heard me shouting, and there was definitely no way he didn't know what it was for.

A cold ass was not how I wanted to spend my lunch break. And yes, that was a thing, even in New Orleans.

Toilet water was a chill not even a heatwave could get rid of.

I threw myself into my chair and glared at him some more. If he knew, he was blatantly ignoring me.

No, there was no if about it.

He knew.

I could see the damn twitching of his perfect little lips, no matter how much he tried to hide it. He wasn't very stealthy.

I ignored his ignorance. I owned superglue. I could make it so that toilet seat would always stay down.

Then we'd see how good his target practice was.

"What are your plans for the day?" Jake asked when I opened my email.

I clicked on the top one. "I was going to find out my superglue. I showered this morning, so my ass doesn't need another wash every time I have to go pee."

He half-snorted, half-coughed in response. "Rule two: put the toilet seat down, right?"

"Right. Consideration is your friend, Mr. Creed. I'm not a nice person when I think somebody doesn't care about my well-being."

"Your ass getting a little wet because I left the toilet seat is not caring? Jesus. It's like living with my sister again."

"You have a sister?"

"Two of them. Sadly."

I peered around the side of my screen. "Then you should have good practice in putting the seat down. And if you can't put the seat down, sit down and tuck it in."

"Tuck it in? It's not a shirt, Melanie."

"Melanie? Whoa, whoa!" I waved my hands and met his eyes. "No. My name is Mellie. The only person who calls me Melanie is my grandmother." And my friends when they were being extra-assholish.

"I'll call you Melanie as long as you call me Mr. Creed."

I blinked at him.

"We appear to have reached an impasse." He grinned, leaning back. He shifted a few times before sitting up straight. "Damn chair."

"Fine. Fine. But the real impasse is you not putting the toilet seat down." I clicked "reply" to the email I was looking over. "Do I need to glue it, or no?"

"No. Please don't. It might be hard explaining that to the cleaning department."

"It really won't be." I typed out the short reply and sent it. "They're all women. They'd take great delight in me doing that."

"I'm beginning to think I'm outnumbered in this building."

I paused, giving him my full attention. "As a rule, yes. But have you ever seen a man clean a toilet?"

"I don't usually look in the mirror as I scrub limescale from the porcelain, no," he replied dryly.

"Interesting." I tilted my head to the side. "You can clean them, but not leave them the way you found them."

"I never know if you're messing with me or if you're deadly serious."

"As a rule, if it comes out of my mouth, I'm serious. I'm an asshole at both ends, you know."

Jake sighed. "You're so lucky you're pretty with a mouth like that."

"What's wrong with my mouth?"

He met my eyes. "Nothing."

I clicked my tongue. "You know what's wrong with yours?"

"What?"

"It lies." I turned my attention back to my screen. All to the tune of his laughter, of course. He was lying. What the truth was, I didn't know; I just knew he wasn't sharing it with me.

"Only when it's appropriate." Jake's lips were fully curved up, and the faint crinkles that framed his eyes only added to the charm of the shine that caught in the sunlight. "Mellie, I have an idea."

I sighed, once again looking at him. "The last time I heard those words, I ended up going for dinner without a bra and flashing random guys."

"Do you make it a habit?"

"Are you aware that I have work to do?"

"Yes." He leaned forward, grinning. "Yes. Are you aware you can tell me to shut up?"

"Yes, but I'm far more curious than I am sensible."

His laughter made goosebumps dance up and down my arms—a wild waltz that ignited a shiver-worthy of making my heart skip a beat. "I have an idea. I think we should have lunch."

I blinked at him. "Have lunch," I stated. "Whatever makes you think that's a good idea?"

He waved his arm. "Close quarters. I think we should get to know each other a little better."

"I think we're plenty acquainted."

"I disagree. So, I booked us a table for lunch."

"I have plans."

"You do. With me." He stood, grabbing his jacket from the back of the chair. "Get up, buttercup. Let's go."

And I did.

Because this was such a great idea.

⸺◦◆◦⸺

"The manager isn't currently available. If she has an issue with her room, find Lillie. That's her job to deal with unless the ceiling has caved in." I pinched the bridge of my nose.

"I can't find her," Jillian said in a hushed tone. "I've tried, but she's not answering when I try to get her."

Jesus. I needed something stronger than an ice Pepsi. "Jillian—you find out the issue, and if you can't help, you get her a free coffee from the bar and run around until you've found Lillie. Or Susanna, if Lillie isn't working. I'm at a business meeting with Mr. Creed, and really, this is basic customer service."

"I know." She pretty much whimpered it. "But she's loud and scary."

"So am I," I replied. "If it isn't resolved in fifteen minutes, call me again, and I'll come back and sort it, but it won't go down well."

"Got it. Bye." She hung up quicker than a bullet leaving a gun.

I shook my head and went back into the café. We hadn't even had a chance to order yet, thanks to the frantic call from the not-so-new girl.

Knowing her, it was probably a broken coffee machine. Why couldn't I get the staff?

I slid back into my seat across from Jake and sighed. "Sorry about that."

He held up a hand, coffee mug firmly in the other. "Don't worry about it. I told her to come back for our order. Problems?"

I shook my head. "We hired some new people not long ago. Some are taking longer to fit in than the others...I don't have a lot of patience."

"No. I couldn't tell."

I picked up my Pepsi and glared at him.

He laughed, setting his coffee mug down. "What was it this time?"

"A minor room issue she apparently couldn't deal with. I told her this was a business meeting and she needed to get on with it or I wouldn't be happy. She ran."

Another laugh.

Man, he laughed a lot.

I hated it.

No, I didn't, but it was easier to say than the alternative.

"You can be scary when you put your foot down. Has anyone told you that?" He flattened his forearms on the table.

"Is this about the no-boob rule again?"

At that moment, the server returned.

Of course, she did.

"Uh," she said, dark eyes flitting between us both, the embarrassment clear even in her dark cheeks. "Do I need to come back?"

"No," Jake said before I could answer. "What do you recommend I have?" he asked me.

"Do you trust me?" I grinned.

"Absolutely not, so I have a feeling I'm going to regret this."

———◦•◦———

Thirty minutes later, Jake held the chicken-nugget-lookalike between his finger and thumb. "Alligator," he said. "This is an alligator?"

"Well, it's not a whole alligator. Just a part of it."

He glanced at it then back at me. "You know, I watched a lot of Peter Pan as a kid. I'm not sure I can eat the Tick-Tock Croc."

"You won't be. It's an *all-ih-gay-ter*," I emphasized. "Not a crocodile."

"What's the difference?"

"The alligator will see you later. The crocodile will see you in a while."

Jake blinked at me. "Oh, well, shit. That cleared it up."

I cough-laughed into my hand. "Don't blame me. You walked right into that one."

"I just don't think I can eat alligator."

I snatched a piece off the plate and popped it into my mouth. As I chewed, I stared at him like a little weirdo. When I was done, I held out my hands. "See? It's good. I promise. It's not slimy or chewy."

He glanced at it. "It's weird."

I leaned forward. "Eat it before I choke you on it."

He threw the piece into his mouth and chewed. His expression went from screwed up to relaxed, and he even raised his eyebrows right before his throat bobbed as he swallowed. "Shit. Do I have to admit that you're right now?"

Grinning, I sat back. "You do."

"It was good."

"Tastes like chicken, right?"

"What if chicken tastes like alligator, and I've been fooled my whole life?"

I held up a hand and pinched the bridge of my nose. "If I wanted deep thoughts, I'd google conspiracy theories. I just want to know if you liked it or not."

"It tastes like chicken," he admitted. "And—"

"No. Chicken does not taste like alligator."

"How do you know?"

I held up my hand for the bill. We were most definitely done here. We'd both had a glass of wine while we'd discussed business before His Royal Handsomeness had decided he wanted to try alligator.

He'd faltered, obviously, but he'd tried it in the end. With a little diva.

The bill was brought over by our server. Jake snatched the bill up before I could so much as twitch in its direction. I glared at him, but all he did was answer with a wide grin that made me want to blush.

He handed her his card, and she went to run it.

"I could argue, but instead, I'll simply say thank you and move on," I said.

"Damn, here I was thinking you'd yell at me. What a shame. Also, you're welcome."

I clutched my hand to my chest. "Me, yell for buying me lunch? I would have if you eating alligator hadn't been so funny."

"Still tastes like chicken."

"Okay." I picked up my purse from the floor and set it on my lap. "I have to get back. Are you going to follow me?"

"You could just wait, and we go together."

"But then I'll have to hear about the alligator, and I have work to do." I pushed the chair back and stood up.

"Here you go, sir." The server brought back his card at that exact moment.

"Thank you." Jake took it and slid it into his wallet before joining me in standing. "There. Look at that. Now we can go together."

"Wonderful," I muttered, pulling my purse straps over my shoulder. "Let's go. We've been gone long enough that there will be a lot of questions."

"Why? Will something have happened?"

"No, the staff are just nosy."

Jake pushed the door open and held it for me to walk through first. When I raised my eyebrow at him, he simply motioned for me to go with a sweep of his hand.

Look at that.

A rare gentleman in the wild.

"Thank you," I muttered.

"You're welcome." He stepped out onto the sidewalk and guided me toward the crossing with his hand on the small of my back. "We need to talk about the staff."

"We do?" I jerked my head around to face him.

He nudged me onto the road to cross with a nod. "Yes. If like you say, there were recent hires who are less than competent, then something has to be done about it."

That didn't sound good.

"Done about it," I echoed.

"I get the impression the previous owner didn't really run the place very well."

"Or at all."

"Or at all," he agreed. "I have a different view of owning the hotel. I plan to be very hands on without taking away from your job. From what I can see, you do your job perfectly."

Oh, gee, that made me feel better about where this conversation was going.

"Mellie?"

I stopped and met his gaze right before we talked into the hotel. "We're not having this conversation where we can be heard. End of."

I walked inside without waiting for his response.

He'd have to do better than that to justify his thought process.

UPSIDE #9: YOU CAN DO WHAT YOU WANT. YOU ALSO HAVE TO DO THE THINGS YOU DON'T WANT TO DO—LIKE PROVIDE YOUR OWN ORGASMS.

Jake joined me in the office around ten minutes after I'd stormed off from him. Unfortunately for him, I was on the phone and returning a call, so he'd have to wait.

Ring, ring.

How could he make the decision to just fire people? He knew nothing about the people who worked here. And they weren't all bad at their jobs, they were just…not wholly competent in all areas.

Neither was I. I only just managed the people side of my job.

Ring, ring.

Was it normal to just fire people when a new owner came in? The previous ones I'd known hadn't. All right, so this was the only job I'd ever known, but still. Wasn't that morally wrong?

These people had families and bills to pay.

He couldn't fire them because he didn't know them.

Ring, ring.

I held the phone to my ear with such harshness it almost hurt. Jake paced back and forth in front of the desk, hands in his pockets, head down, eyes on the floor. Was he thinking about the bluntness he'd just used? How unreasonable the idea seemed?

I couldn't work with this man. I just couldn't. And it wasn't even about the boobs thing. It was just…everything.

He was too attractive.

Too strong-willed.

Too-pig-headed and stubborn.

Just like me. And there wasn't enough room in this hotel for two stubborn idiots.

I sighed as the call rolled to voicemail. I left a quick message with a time frame to call back and hung up. Jake was still pacing. Up and down the office like he was on autopilot.

I leaned back in my chair and stared at him. "You're just going to fire people without bothering to get to know them? You haven't even been here a week. The only person you've spoken to more than twice is me."

He stopped, sighed, and looked at me. "Are you going to listen to me?"

"Listen to what? How you're going to fire half my staff?" I stood up and put my hands on my hips.

"You have a real problem with authority, don't you?"

"Actually, no. I get on with authority just fine. Unless the authority is being an asshole."

Jake walked toward me and tapped my nose. "Sit down, Melanie, before I fire *you* for running that pretty little mouth of yours."

Said mouth dropped open at his bold statement. "My name is Mellie. And if you tap my nose again, you won't have to fire me, because I'll kick you on my way out."

His lips twitched to the side. "Calm down, spitfire. If you'd be quiet for five minutes, you'll see there's more to my plan than just randomly pointing at people and firing them. Now, are you going to listen?"

"I—"

"Nope." He cupped my chin and pressed his thumb against my lips, shutting me up. "That's not listening."

"I was going to say I'd listen," I murmured against his thumb. "But you stopped me."

He just stared at me for a moment. I hoped he'd remove his thumb, but no. He didn't. He kept hold of my jaw, his fingers digging into my skin and making it tingle, and talked again.

"You know there's a big refurb happening. Part of my plans is an entire overhaul of everything, including staffing. And you're right. I don't know any of the staff or what they're doing, but what I do know is that you're not happy about some of them."

Well, that wasn't a lie.

"Do you do staff meetings?"

I didn't answer. His thumb was still on my mouth.

He raised his eyebrows.

I glanced down.

He got the hint.

I shivered and stepped back. "Mostly managerial meetings. It's the job of the departmental managers to hold regular meetings with their staff. I know Rosa, who heads cleaning, has meetings twice a week. Lillie does it three times. Off the top of my head."

"How often do you hold meetings?"

"Once a week. It doesn't need to be any more often. It's mostly to go over rosters, orders, special events, things like that."

Jake nodded. "When's your next meeting?"

"Uh…" I picked up the planner from the desk. "Tomorrow morning."

He perched on the corner of my desk, taking the planner from me. "I want to be there. New ownership means new rules. If you're not happy with the staff, neither am I. As of tomorrow, all staff—including management—will be under review. If in two weeks, they're deemed not good enough, they'll be given a one-week notice of unemployment."

I swallowed. "Even the managers?"

"Who is responsible for training the staff?"

"The departmental managers," I said gently.

"So, if their staff aren't up to scratch, they're not being trained properly. Like when I got here on Monday, and you were doing the bar order. The manager was on vacation—a stupid idea during Mardi Gras—and the staff member who should have been doing it was unable to." He scratched the back of his neck. "You have enough to do without picking up the slack of another department."

"How did you know all that?"

"I smiled at Lillie, and she folded like a wet piece of paper."

I let go of a long breath. "Of course. Look, it wasn't a big deal. It was busy. And if it weren't for the fact Quinn's sister was getting married, she never would have had this week off."

"It is a big deal." He folded his arms across his chest. "If you walk into a coffee shop and they get your order wrong, you'd complain. If the same staff member got it wrong every day or needed help to use the machine, you'd think they need to be fired."

I opened my mouth to argue, but I couldn't. He was right.

"I'm not unreasonable, Mellie. But I'm also not a horrible person for wanting to have the best possible staff working for me. This building is literally my entire inheritance. I'm living with my cousin, for the love of God. There's nothing worse than hearing his personal pornstars going at it in his bedroom every night."

I bit the corner of my bottom lip and fought a smile.

"If I didn't have to make this hotel a success, I would be living on my own. In peace."

"It could be worse."

"He asked me last night if I wanted to join them. It really couldn't."

This time, I couldn't fight it. I let my lips curve into a smile, and I laughed, too. Hell, even Jake couldn't fight a low laugh of his own.

"Fine. As long as the length of employment and willingness to undergo re-training is considered," I finally relented. "But I'm not the one delivering the news about the review, you are."

He held out his hands. "What is this? Good cop, bad cop?"

"Yes," I said, putting the planner back where it belonged. "Because I'm the nice one they all like, and you're the mean new guy."

"Way to endear my employees to me."

"Judging by your relationship with Lillie so far, all you have to do is smile and the women here practically melt into their panties."

He quirked a brow. "Do you do that when I smile?"

Yes. "In your dreams, New Guy. I'd rather melt into quicksand."

He stood, his gray eyes seeing through the lie. "You're a terrible liar."

I folded my arms across my chest and met his eyes. "That's a matter of opinion. Now, do you know how to run a staff meeting, or do you need me to draw up a plan for you?"

He grinned wolfishly. "If I need you to, does that mean you won't do anything for me?"

I narrowed my eyes. "What do you want me to do?"

"I told my cousin you're the manager. He wants to know if he can have the number for your friend with "the huge knockers.""

"Peyton? Oh God, no. If I give out her number, she'll shoot me." I paused. "She's picky. If he has a dick pic, that's a whole other story."

"A dick pic?"

I opened the top drawer of my desk and pulled out a small business card with "Pick A Dick" on the front, the 'i' in 'dick' shaped like a penis. "Um, here."

Slowly, Jake took the card from me. Pinching the corner between his finger and thumb, he scanned the card and read, "Pick A Dick. Dick pics required."

"The website is on the back." I twirled my finger in a circle. "She runs a hook-up website. She basically spends her life looking at dicks and matching men to women looking for specific things."

"What is this? Tinder on crack?"

"That's pretty much it, yeah."

"Except she wants the dick pics?"

"They're required," I said. "You can't send an application if you're a guy and don't attach a dick pic."

He peered up from the card and looked at me. "I don't really know how to respond to this."

"Yeah, well you should have seen her dad's face when she announced it. Her grandma offered to sign up. Actually, it might have been her grandma that scared him."

Jake nodded slowly and tucked the card into his back pocket. "Well, if anyone has a plethora of dick pics on their phone, it's Sam."

"There are people who don't have a plethora of dick pics on their phones?"

"I can honestly say I've never once taken a photo of my cock."

"Why? Can the camera not see it?" The words came out before I could stop them.

Jake stared at me for a moment. Something warred in his eyes—amusement and restraint, as if he wanted to reply but couldn't.

I swallowed as he stood up and took one step closer to me. He reached out, fingers trailing across my temple as he pushed my blond hair behind my ear.

"No, spitfire," he said in a low, cool voice. "It wouldn't fit on the screen."

I drew in a sharp breath through my nose. His words, his touch, the warmth of his breath skittering across my cheek—it made me shiver. Desire tickled down to the pit of my belly, and Jake bit back a chuckle as he released me.

My eyes dropped momentarily to his crotch before I yanked my attention away and stared at an empty photo frame on the bookshelf behind me.

"I'm going to endear myself to my employees before tomorrow." He kept his eyes on me the entire time. "I'd really appreciate if you could focus on a review plan for me."

I put as much annoyance in my glare as I could, but obviously, it was nowhere near enough, because his laugh echoed down the hall, even when he was well out of sight of me.

That bastard.

<hr />

Peyton: *Is he sending a dick pic?*
Chloe: *Don't you get enough of those?*
Peyton: *Nothing I'm interested in.*
Me: *I've had enough talk about dicks today. I was just giving you a heads up.*
Peyton: *Why? Are you schmoozing your new boss?*
Me: *I don't want to talk about my boss.*
Peyton: *If you don't want him…*
Chloe: *Don't you have a date tonight, Pey?*
Peyton: *The little d doesn't always equal the big D, you know that.*
Me: *I don't want to be friends with you people anymore.*

I closed the group chat and put my phone face-down on the desk. I was supposed to have left work roughly two hours ago, but that was before a fight had broken out in one of our hotel rooms and the police showed up.

Don't cheat on your girlfriend. She will smash your head with a vase, then throw a shoe at the girl you're mid-fuck with.

In the hotel room you're sharing with your girlfriend.

Lillie and I decided to keep our opinions about him deserving the vase over the head while we spoke to the police. I'd sent her home, but it'd been so wild for the hour this all happened that I still hadn't come down from the high.

So, that's why I was still sitting in my office with my feet up on the desk, and my shoes were strewn across the floor.

I was tired and I was hungry, but I was still buzzing like crazy.

I was also totally icked out because I hated blood, and Mr. Cheater had been covered in it.

Not only had I had to get the room basically steamed by the maids, I'd had to reassure all our customers that it was a one-time thing and give them all vouchers for a free alcoholic drink.

Nobody was bringing me one, though, were they?

I leaned right back in the chair and closed my eyes. The leftover adrenaline was slowly beginning to subside, and the more my head cleared, the more resigned I became to the fact that I'd be ordering dinner in and throwing out the chicken I'd left to defrost.

This wasn't how I'd planned on spending my Friday night. Never mind I'd planned to spend it braless and sans pants, eating on my sofa in front of trashy reality TV.

Three light knocks sounded at the door.

I opened my eyes and rolled my head to the side. "Yes?"

The hinges squeaked as the door opened. Jake walked through, a big pizza box balanced on his hand. He lifted it up. "I thought you'd be hungry."

"How did—never mind. The cops called you?"

He closed the door behind him and nodded. "Not long after they arrived here. I've already been down to speak to them and confirm pressing charges for the damage done to the hotel room." He pushed my keyboard and mouse to the side and set the pizza down. "I called here to see if everything was okay and Lillie said you were still here and hadn't eaten, so I stopped by the pizza place. And the bar on the way back here." He placed a bottle of white wine on the desk along with two glasses.

I hadn't even seen him holding that.

"Thank you." I smiled. "You're good at feeding me. Maybe sharing an office won't be so bad after all."

His lips curved to the side. "Food is the way to your heart. Got it."

I was too exhausted to respond. I wasn't even tired—if I went to bed, there'd be no way I could sleep. I was simply exhausted.

"Here. Eat, and then tell me why you're still here this late although it's all been dealt with." He opened the box, and the scent of hot, melted cheese and pepperoni reached me.

My stomach rumbled.

I couldn't even be embarrassed. I snatched up one of the slices and bit into the end of it. Apparently, I was starving. I hadn't eaten since we'd had lunch, and that was now eight hours ago. I'd barely drunk anything in the last few, so downing half the glass of wine halfway through my first slice of pizza probably wasn't my best idea.

Ah, who was I kidding? Wine was always a good idea.

We both ate in silence. Well, I mostly ate. Jake sat on his phone, swiping and tapping across the screen until I was done. Although I'd been starving, three pieces had been the sweet spot.

I wiped my mouth with a napkin then scrunched it up and threw it into the pizza box. A sigh escaped me before I could stop it, and I leaned right back in my chair and threw my forearm over my eyes.

"What happened? The police could only give me a vague timeline because they hadn't interviewed everyone yet, but I've seen the room already."

I let my arm fall and met his eyes. "I'm not sure how it started. Actually, that's a lie. It started because some idiot brought a random girl back to the hotel when he was here with his girlfriend." I pulled my hair out of the ponytail it'd been in all day and ran my fingers through it until it hung loosely over my shoulders. "The general idea and smashed vodka bottle in the room tells me they were pretty drunk."

"Yeah. I think they took her to the hospital to evaluate her because she passed out at the station."

I rolled my eyes. "There you go, then. Stupid choices all around. Anyway, the maids were cleaning the room next door ready for an early check-in tomorrow when the girlfriend showed up."

Jake nodded slowly. "They said it was something like that."

"Yeah, well the worst part is that it spilled out into the hall where a family was just returning back to their room. Their children saw the whole thing, including her screaming blue murder at him and using cuss words I didn't know existed."

"Ah, shit."

"I'd use a stronger word. I know a few new ones now." I picked up my wine glass and let it dangle in my hand, cupping the main bit. "As well as having to offer discounts to every hotel resident at the bar by the way of a free drink, I had to give her one night free off her bill by way of apology."

"Did she accept it?"

"After her husband told her that punching a drunk person would get her arrested."

"Usually, I'm against violence, but that would have been acceptable."

I tilted my wine glass in his direction before taking a sip. "So, that's why I'm still here. I had to inform all the staff what had happened and that any questions should be directed to management. I pulled the meeting forward tomorrow so everyone is prepared, then I had to people and reassure everyone it was over and it was a personal misunderstanding."

Jake's eyes searched my face. They flit up and down, from the frown marring my forehead to the way I had my lips downturned. I didn't need to look in the mirror to know what my expression looked like.

I could feel it.

Like I said, I was exhausted. I wanted my bed, even though I knew I wouldn't sleep.

"Mellie...Are you all right?" The concern in his voice trickled warmly over my skin.

"I'm fine. Honestly. I'm just tired." I set the empty wine glass down. "I can't begin to imagine how much damage that incident may have caused."

"It's all fixable."

"I don't mean financially. I mean to the hotel. Once the local media get hold of it..."

He leaned forward. "You're tired. I can handle the meeting tomorrow. You go home and come in later."

"I am tired, but it's fine."

Jake stood and held out one hand. "Come on. I'll take you home."

"I'm fine. Really. I have some paperwork to do."

He walked around the desk, hand still out. "Let's go."

"I just said—"

He grabbed my hand and yanked me up, then scanned the floor for my shoes. Letting go of my hand, he picked up the shoes and handed them to me. "Put these ball-scaring stilettos on and let's go. I'm not arguing with you. I'm taking you home, and you can come in late."

"Fine." I took the shoes from him. "You can take me home, but I'll be here at seven."

"We'll continue the last part of that in a minute."

I'm sure we would.

I would also win.

I slipped my feet into the heels, grabbed my things, and allowed him to steer me out of the office. He locked it behind us, then cupped my elbow and guided me through the hotel. I waved a half-hearted goodbye to Lillie on the front desk before leaving with Jake.

He'd parked in the next street over. I couldn't even take a minute to enjoy the sleek beauty of his Audi. Instead, I allowed him to open the door so I could sit on the cream, leather passenger seat and spear my heels into the mat on the floor in front of me.

Jake closed the door and walked around to the driver side. He said nothing as he got in and started the car. I was thankful for his silence. This week had started hellacious and, apparently, was going to end that way.

From my boss knowing what my boobs looked like to seconds away from a potential murder scene, I was one hundred percent done.

Okay.

The murder scene thing might have been an exaggeration, but not much of one.

Given another five minutes and some privacy, we could have had a haunting on our hands.

Hey, it was New Orleans…

"What are you thinking?" Jake glanced over at me at a red light.

"That we almost had a resident ghost at the hotel."

"You think?"

"That she could have murdered him or that he'd have left a ghost behind?"

"The ghost thing. Do you believe in them?"

I shifted, turning my head to look at him. "I live in New Orleans. Of course, I believe in ghosts. The entire history of this city is steeped in ghosts and hauntings. Do you know nothing about it here?"

"No." He pulled away, glancing at me once more. "I told you, I've never been here. I don't know a lot. Especially not about ghosts."

"You should do a ghost tour. Apparently, they're great for tourists."

"You've never done one? And I'm not a tourist. I'm a resident. Technically."

"Why would I do a ghost tour? I've lived here my whole life. I've heard all the tour stories and then some." I paused, tucking hair away from my face. "And you're an almost resident. Until you can eat our food without wincing, eat the head of a crawfish, and accept this city is haunted as fuck, you're an almost resident."

"All right. I think I can do all that, but I need a ghost tour."

"I bet Brittany can find you a ghost tour for this weekend."

He slid his gaze toward me quickly. "I think you should find me a ghost tour."

"Wait. Why me?"

"You're the one who brought up ghosts."

"Still, she's the one who knows all the best tours. She literally advises on them and books them as part of her job. Get her to do it."

We pulled onto my street and miraculously, he was able to pull into an empty spot on the side of the road behind my car.

"You brought up the ghosts. You find me a tour." He undid his seatbelt and killed the engine, then flashed me that disarming grin. "Please."

I stared at him for a moment before I relented. "Fine. I'll do my best."

"You're coming with me."

"I'm damn well not." At that, I got out of the car and dug through my purse to find my keys.

"Aw, come on, Mellie." Jake followed me, hands out at his sides, his bottom lip jutted right out. "Why not? It'll be fun. You know this city better than I do. I'm still using GPS, for fuck's sake." He pointed at the GPS embedded in the dashboard. "I'll get lost on my way there."

"I feel like this is bribery. Why don't you bring all the staff and make it a morale-boosting trip?" I finally retrieved my keys from the depths of Coach leather and pulled them out with a flourish.

"Because that sounds like my idea of hell," he admitted. "I don't like people."

"You just bought a hotel." I stared at him.

He raised his eyebrows. "You don't like people and you manage the hotel."

"Yes, well, I was a naïve little teenager happy to have independence when I got the job. Working with people has jaded me against them."

"So, in a ghost tour, the people are all dead."

"Not true. There are groups of like fifteen people. They're definitely living."

He leaned against the stone column that held up the balcony just off my bedroom, folded his arms across his chest, and smirked at me. "You just sound like you don't want to be alone with me."

"I've spent half my day alone with you. There's just a chance I don't like ghosts."

"How can you live here your whole life and not like ghosts?"

"All right, first," I held up a finger, "It's New Orleans, not Amityville."

He snort-laughed.

"And I happen to believe that a lot of the stories are fabricated."

"I feel like you're making excuses."

"I feel like you're doing your best to talk me into it."

Jake paused, then nodded. "Absolutely, I am. Will it kill you to take me on a ghost tour? After all I've done for you this week? Donuts, lunch, pizza…"

I clicked my tongue. "That's low, Jake. That's real low."

He grinned, still leaning against the column. "Look, it's either you take me on a ghost tour, or I'm going to insist you come in late to work tomorrow."

"That's even lower!"

"I'm not messing with you, Melanie."

"I don't like your attitude, Mr. Creed."

"Touché," he muttered, pushing off the column and walking toward me. "Well? Will it kill you?"

I swallowed and glanced away before the intensity of his gaze made me meet his eyes. "Maybe. Some ghosts are violent."

He smiled, his full lips twitching. He reached up and scratched the side of his jaw, and my fingers itched with the fleeting desire to see if the stubble that darkened his jaw was as spiky and tickly as it looked.

"Don't worry. I'll protect you." The smile widened, turning wolfish, and the glint in his eye matched that, too.

This sounded like a terrible idea.

"You're going to keep annoying me about it until I agree, aren't you?" My grip on my key tightened, and it cut into my palm. "I can see it in your eyes."

He didn't say anything. Just stared at me with that stupid grin on his face.

"Fine." I threw my hand in the air and almost dropped my keys. "Fine. I'll take you on a damn ghost tour, but I'm going to bitch and complain the entire time. Are you okay with that?"

He hooked his finger under my chin, his smile still unwavering. "I think I'll be able to cope with it."

UPSIDE #10: THE ONLY GHOST IN YOUR LIFE IS THE MEMORY OF HAVING TO PICK UP SOMEONE ELSE'S DIRTY SOCKS.

It was dark. Luckily it wasn't cold, but the dark was enough for me. The only good thing about this stupid-ass tour was the fact I got two free cocktails for my troubles.

And, apparently, there was a bar stop halfway through.

God bless New Orleans law that let me drink on the street.

Jake nudged my elbow with his as we followed our group, hanging a little to the back. "She seems fierce," he said, nodding in the direction of our tour guide.

That was one word for her. The second she'd stepped in front of our group and smashed her cane against the ground, she'd gained our full attention. And, not that Jake wanted to admit it, but she'd got a hint of fear out of us all, too.

That, and her name was Mistress Stella.

I was more afraid of her than the potential ghosts—and how I kept staring at Jake's arms in his black polo shirt.

It was easier than you'd think in the dim street lights.

That, or I was looking too damn hard.

"Mellie? Are you paying attention?"

I blinked at him. "As a rule, probably not."

The fall-out from the craziness of Friday night hadn't been too bad, but it'd just been a busy day all around. Except for the meeting, I hadn't even seen Jake until he turned up on my doorstep half an hour early.

At least, this time, I'd already had my bra on.

Progress.

"I said she seems fierce." He nodded once again over to Stella. "She looks like she could whip some ass with that cane of hers."

"I might buy one for work. That might make the review process a little more intimidating."

He peered down at me, lifting his cup to his mouth. "You're about as intimidating as a newborn kitten. No offense."

"They have claws, you know."

He took my hand in his and looked at my nails. "Yeah, ouch. I can see how they'd hurt a guy."

I opened my mouth to respond, but at that moment, Stella stopped and knocked her cane against the sidewalk. We were standing on the corner of a small sidewalk right next to St. Louis Cathedral, and when I looked at the building she was about to tell us about, my eyebrows rose.

I knew this story.

"Legend," Stella said, "of the Octoroon Mistress."

Nobody said a word.

"What's an octoroon?" Jake muttered in my ear.

Not quietly enough.

"Excellent question." Stella brandished her cane in his direction, and he stood bolt upright.

I bit the inside of my cheek.

"Octoroon was the term used in the eighteen-hundreds for people who were one-eighth black and the rest white. Now, it was forbidden for these people to pursue a relationship with the elite creoles who inhabited the city, but the gentlemen were often attracted to the young ladies because they were beautiful." She swung her cane up onto her shoulder. "In the house behind us," she motioned with her hand toward it, "Lived a young octoroon lady we know as Julie. She was in love with a wealthy Frenchman, and while they lived together, she was not to be seen or heard by his equally wealthy friends."

"Sounds like a bastard," Jake muttered to me.

"For months she begged him to marry her, but he refused. Their social standing was different. He couldn't marry her, until one day, he devised a test." She paced back and forth a few times. "He was going to play a card game downstairs with some friends, and he told Julie that while he was entertaining his friends, she was to strip off her clothing and wait for him on the roof."

Jake's eyebrows shot up.

"Did she do it?" someone in the group asked.

Stella bobbed her head, her bright-blonde curls bouncing with the movement. "She did. It was cold and damp in December, but she was desperate to prove she loved him. When her lover went to bed hours later, he didn't possibly think she would be on the roof, but she wasn't in bed."

A couple of people gasped.

"When he reached the roof, he found her naked and frozen in the corner; her dead body curled up as she was still waiting for him."

"Well, shit," Jake said under his breath.

I peered over at him. Never had I seen a grown man so interested in anything except football or porn.

"What an asshole!" someone said.

Stella nodded their way in apparent agreement. "Now, he had grown to care for Julie and truly loved her. The story says he fell into a deep depression and some say he died of a broken heart several months later."

"He deserved that," someone else said.

"If you look on the roof on the right night, you can see Julie's ghost, still naked, walking back and forth across the edge of the roof, waiting for her lover." She paused. "Her ghost is so real, the police department have received calls about her. They used to come to check it at first, but now, when they hear the address, they tell the caller they'll get there as soon as they can. They don't come because they know the naked lady in Royal Street is none other than Julie."

She stopped talking, leaving our entire group in silence with only the echoes of the Quarter and surrounding streets as a background noise. Then, "Any questions?"

There were questions.

"Is that true? The ghost thing?" Jake leaned into me, moving out of the way so someone could walk behind him.

"Depends on who you ask. Some people are real certain they've seen her, but others think it's just another story. The city is full of them. It can be hard to tell which ones are true and which ones are just for attention," I replied.

"Have you seen her?"

I shook my head. "Chloe claims she thinks she saw someone on the roof."

"Do you believe her?"

"Sure. I mean, I think you have to be looking for it to see it. I've grown up with the stories my whole life, so I just accept them as true. Some of the things my grandma used to tell me were terrifying."

"Like what?"

Stella interrupted our conversation to tell us to move on to the next stop on the tour.

I turned, but there was no grip on my flats, and I slipped on a damp cobblestone. I squealed. Jake grabbed hold of me with one arm, wrapping it tightly around my waist so I didn't go ass down onto the street.

"I'm starting to think you're a walking liability," he murmured, lips way too close to my ear for my liking. "And I really, really need to invest in that bubble wrap."

I coughed, blushing, and wriggled my way out of his grasp. "It's fine. I'm fine. Thank you. It's wet."

He raised an eyebrow at me.

"The stone. The stone was wet." I cleared my throat. "We should catch up."

He held out his arm. "Fine, but you're holding my arm. I don't want to be responsible for you getting into a fight with the sidewalk."

I glanced down at the muscled arm he was offering me. I couldn't take that. I'd be distracted by the bicep all night.

"Mellie. Hurry up, or we'll lose the group."

Looking forward told me he was right—they were almost out of sight.

Against my better judgment, I looped my hand into the crook of his elbow and held onto him. He rested his arm against his body, tucking my hand right against him and almost trapping it in place.

I tried to focus on not falling on the cobblestones. Really, I did, but it wasn't my fault that heat slowly trickled across my skin from where my fingers were resting on his arm. It wasn't my fault that heat carried a bolt of electricity that almost made me feel like I was on fire, like all the hairs on my body were now standing to attention in shock.

It wasn't my fault that the way my arm kept bumping his meant that eye contact was out of the question.

And it definitely wasn't my fault that this new, close proximity to hard, defined upper arms combined with the hint of rich aftershave and mint made my heart beat a little bit faster.

I was in the middle of New Orleans, and the only scent I could truly focus on was him.

Lavender on his shirt.

Mint on his breath.

The woody, musky aftershave on his neck.

I couldn't focus a bit on the next story Stella told us. All I could do was make sure I was looking anywhere other than at Jake, because this schoolgirl crush I had going on was a little more than just that.

In the middle of the French Quarter, I admitted something to myself.

I was wildly attracted to Jacob Creed.

I was wildly attracted to my boss. To the man who literally had control over a part of my life. To a man who'd seen my boobs and declared them lovely.

Who looked at my signature clumsiness with nothing more than amusement—not annoyance, like so many other people had and would do.

A man who held doors for me, bought me dinner, and refused to let me walk on cobblestones without taking his arm.

All right, so the last was for my own safety—and probably that of others, too, let's be honest—but still.

He was a gentleman.

He's also your boss, you daydreaming moron.

Ah, damn the smart, rational part of my mind.

I shook off that line of thought before I got so far down it I'd drown and not come back for any kind of air. I was definitely in trouble if I didn't get myself under control.

We moved to the next place on the tour, the Lalaurie Mansion. Even Jake had to have heard of this one. I didn't know many tourists who came here who didn't know.

"What happened here?" he asked, dipping his head as Stella introduced the building to us and everyone but him seemed to know it.

"You know nothing about this city, do you?"

"I tried to tell you…"

I sighed. "Haven't you ever watched American Horror Story? The third season is based on witchcraft and covens here."

He simply turned his head and blinked at me.

I blinked back.

Man. Our faces were close together.

I cleared my throat and looked away.

"Madame Delphine LaLaurie. LaLaurie Mansion." Stella smacked her lips together and adjusted her tan hat. "It's claimed this house is the most haunted in North America." The street lights flickered above us, and I rolled my eyes. Great timing.

"Born Marie Delphine Macarty…" I trailed off my attention as Stella began the backstory of one of the most notorious women in the city's history. This was the reason I hadn't wanted to come on the tour—not because New Orleans wasn't fascinating, but because I knew all this and more.

Instead of listening, I ran my gaze across the huge house on the corner. One of the windows was boarded up, and the cast iron railings that wrapped around the first-floor balcony was decorated with a handful of flower boxes. The orange flowers and greenery trailed over the sides of the boxes, swaying in the gentle breeze.

I tucked my hair behind my ear. I'd heard it all before, from the young slave girl who supposedly fell off the roof after being whipped by Madame LaLaurie to the fire that broke out and revealed the torture of numerous slaves.

Apparently, though, Jake really hadn't. He watched, mesmerized, as Stella dramatized everything with the inflections in her voice and the odd hand gesture. She stuck to the classic story, none of the embellishment of fiction or Hollywood.

I liked that.

It was more authentic that way.

And I could barely stop looking at Jake. There was something…endearing, about his interest. About how his gray eyes flickered almost silver in the dim lights on the quieter street. How his jaw twitched, and his lips curved down when the story got gruesome.

How he felt standing next to me…

"I'm starting to rethink moving here," he murmured, still staring at the mansion.

I looked up at Jake and quietly laughed. "Don't worry. Nobody skins anyone alive here now. At least, not that I know of."

He jerked his head around and stared at me.

"Any questions?" Stella asked, scanning the group.

"Yes," Jake answered. "Is it time to stop for a beer yet?"

Stella grinned. "You have fifteen minutes. The bar is right there." She pointed to the building a few feet away from us.

"Perfect."

ELEVEN

UPSIDE #11: THE ONLY PERSON YOU HAVE TO EXPLAIN THINGS TO IS YOURSELF. LIKE WHY YOU HAVEN'T DONE LAUNDRY FOR A WEEK.

"I told you this city was haunted."

Jake shook his head. "The vampire thing is fucking weird. Maybe I can handle the torturous ghosts, but vampires?"

I sucked my frozen cocktail up through the straw. The ghost tour had finished almost an hour ago, and we'd ducked into a small bar just off Bourbon Street so he could wrap his head around it.

It didn't seem to be going well.

"Is now a good time to tell you that we have an active vampire population in the city?"

He blinked at me. "There is never a good time to tell anybody that."

"Oh, okay. Well, there's an active vampire population in New Orleans."

His lips flattened and spread into a grimace. "I don't want to know, but at the same time..."

"Curiosity killed the cat."

"Good thing I'm closer to a lion than a cat. Go ahead. Tell me. I'll only Google it and get stories to give a tougher man than me nightmares for the next six years."

I bit back a laugh and looked up at him through my lashes. "Okay. It's not that crazy. I don't think. They don't like…Ugh. It's weird when you say it out loud. Some drink blood, and others do some psychic shit to get energy."

"They drink real blood? Human blood?"

"And animal." I paused and bit the inside of my cheek. "The general idea of it is that they need energy from somewhere other than where humans get it. Some drink blood, some do psychic or astral stuff, and others have sex."

"I'm so confused." Jake frowned. "This doesn't…bother…anyone?"

I shrugged a shoulder. "New Orleans is a weird place. We're tons of different cultures mixed together, and half our history is based on the paranormal. They don't bother us. They're not, like, chasing us down and attacking us in dark alleys. It's all…consensual."

"People allow other people to drink their blood?"

"I sense that bothers you more than the whole drinking it thing."

"No. No, it doesn't. I'm trying to understand one thing at a time."

I laughed and propped my head up on my hand. "I don't understand it, and I've never really tried to. But trust me, we have a lot of weird in New Orleans, but at least the vampires aren't throwing vases at each other's heads."

He tipped his cup of beer toward me with an incline of his head. "True. For all the eccentricities in this city, humans are by far the weirdest."

At least we agreed on something.

"I didn't get a chance to ask you. How are you after last night?"

I put my drink down and shrugged. "I'm fine. I managed to sleep well, so after the mutterings and complaints about the employee review system that starts tomorrow, it was a good day."

He almost winced, but he had the good grace to look sheepish. After all, he'd basically dropped the news and ran, leaving me to deal with the questions. Sure, he'd had an appointment with his lawyer, but that wasn't the point.

I was not amused at his bullshit.

"Sorry about that," he said. "We had to make a couple of urgent changes to the contract with the construction company. I couldn't get out of it."

"It's fine. Mostly the newest members of staff complained to the managers who relayed it to me. I told them I'd take their concerns to the boss because I had nothing to do with the idea." I widened my eyes innocently and sipped my drink.

Jake raised his eyebrows. "Wow. You're really throwing me under the bus as the bad cop, aren't you?"

"Me? No."

"And after I bought you donuts, too."

"You made me go on the stupid ghost tour. Your donut argument is irrelevant."

"It won't be if I buy you donuts tomorrow, too."

"My pants would rather you didn't buy any more. The button is resisting."

"So, don't wear pants."

I blinked at him. "My skirts are joining the resistance of the pants. If I eat any more donuts, everyone will be asking me who the father is."

Jake burst out laughing. "Tell them it's me and really freak them out."

"That would get back to my grandmother in a heartbeat, and she'd have you on one knee in the next. Don't even go there."

"I don't know. Can you cook? I'm not that great at it. I'd marry someone solely based on their ability to feed me."

"How did we go from vampires from this?"

He pushed his cup to the side then leaned his forearms on the table, wearing a stupid grin on his face that made my stomach flip. "I believe it started when you glossed over me essentially telling you that pants are unnecessary."

"No, I understood what you were saying. I simply chose the professional response. You know—since we work together?"

Something flashed in his eyes, and his grin changed from wide and bright to a slow, sexy smirk. "Right. Do you usually take your bosses on ghost tours?"

"No, but then they don't usually bribe me with donuts, either, so you know. It's a trade-off."

"Hey, look, it worked, didn't it? We both won here."

"I had to listen to ninety minutes of things I already knew while walking. The only thing I won at was drinking." Which was becoming a problem since the previous week, I'd noticed. "Talking of which…" I held up my cup. "This is empty, and I have to be at work at eight tomorrow. It's already past my bedtime."

Jake checked his watch and nodded. "You're right. It's getting late. We should go."

We both got up from the table, leaving our cups there. It was dark, and the city was bursting with people. We'd barely stepped outside the bar when we were almost knocked over by a couple of drunk people.

And by we, I mean I was nearly knocked over, because why would it happen to Jake when Captain Calamity here is around?

Without a word—but his smirk firmly in place—he grabbed my hand and hooked it through his elbow once more. I couldn't even argue with it. Not that I minded. I'd spent enough time hanging off his arm tonight, so what was another twenty minutes as he walked me home?

That'd already been cleared up, and I hadn't dared argue with him. Not that I would—it was Saturday night in New Orleans, after all. It wasn't exactly safe.

We walked the streets in silence, slowly moving farther and farther away from the craziness of the Quarter and the surrounding area. It went from bar to bar and shouting and screaming to the odd bar mixed in with eclectic tourist-type shops.

From crazy to calm.

I breathed in the fresher air now we were away from the hustle and bustle. It was so quiet here, and I felt so much more relaxed than I was back in the Quarter.

Well, I usually did. Tonight, it felt weird. Weird because I was too close to Jake, yet I couldn't bring myself to pull my arm from his.

It was because of the cracked sidewalk. I could catch my toe and slip at any point, couldn't I?

Yes, yes, I could. It was nothing to do with how comfortable it was to have my skin against his and the security of him right next to me.

I didn't like it. I didn't like it at all. Even the silence was comfortable, and as someone who generally didn't stop talking, it was alien.

Truth was, I didn't want to talk. I didn't want to break this moment.

Not that we were having a moment.

What even was a moment?

Not this, that was for sure.

"So, the vampire thing," Jake said, glancing down a small alley. "They're not gonna jump me out of an alleyway?"

I side-eyed him. "Would you like *me* to walk *you* home?"

He chuckled. "No, but I will call a taxi. Just in case." He winked at me as we turned onto my street. "Better safe than sorry."

"They're not Dracula. They're not going to bleed you dry. They're about as scary as Edward Cullen."

"Who's that?"

I stopped at the bottom of the steps that lead to my small porch. "Never mind," I replied, shaking my head, then turned and walked up my steps. He followed me up the few steps and pulled his phone out.

"Just calling now." He waved it and dialed while I dug in my cross-body purse for my keys. I unlocked the door while he called and got one booked to come and get him from here. "It's gonna be a few minutes. Do you mind if I wait here?"

"No, it's fine." I put my purse just inside the door and left the door cracked open a little. I leaned against the door frame. "Well, I hate to admit it, but I kinda had fun tonight."

Jake raised his eyebrows, leaning himself against the pillar opposite me. "Really? You've done nothing but complain all night."

"I started having fun when I realized you're afraid of vampires."

"I'm not afraid of vampires. I'm...apprehensive."

"Apprehensive," I echoed. "Sounds like a bullshit way of admitting you're scared."

He held his arms out. "What do I have to do to prove I'm not afraid of one?"

I raised an eyebrow. "You could tell me you're not afraid and make it believable. Your twitching eye doesn't help your cause at all."

Jake immediately clapped his hand to his temple, and I burst out laughing. I was totally bluffing, and he'd fallen for it. I didn't even know his tell for lying—as far as I knew, I'd never seen him lie.

"Fucking hell." He dropped his hand and laughed, too. "All right, you win this round. But I'm warning you— tomorrow, I'm bringing two donuts to work, and they'll both be for me."

My jaw dropped. "That's just cruel."

He held his hands out as the tell-tale glare of a taxi light rounded the corner at the far end of the street. "You play the vampire card, I play the donut card. All is fair in war and war."

I pouted, glaring at him. "You're so lucky that's your taxi, or I'd kick your ass."

He grinned, pushing off the pillar. "Big talk for someone six inches shorter than me."

I kept on glaring.

He kept on grinning. He closed the distance between us and tugged on a lock of my hair. "Thank you for tonight. I had fun. Even if you didn't."

"I just told you I had fun!"

"Goodnight, Mellie." He dipped his head down.

I turned my head.

His lips touched mine.

I froze.

Heat flooded right through me. My heart thundered against my ribs, and I squeezed my eyes tight shut.

Oh, my God.

He was kissing me.

I was kissing him.

What was happening?

It lasted only a second, but it felt like time had stopped. A thousand things whirred through my brain, things I couldn't grab hold of and comprehend, because how was I supposed to know he was going in for a cheek kiss and how could he know I was about to turn to go inside and oh God how had this happened?

We both pulled apart. My cheeks burned bright red, and I stared stupidly at him for a moment, looking into those damn gray eyes of his.

"Okay, thanks, goodnight!" The words left me so fast they practically became just one word, and I turned faster than I ever had to my front door. My foot caught on the bottom of the frame, and I almost fell through the door instead of running through it.

I was pretty sure I heard him chuckle as I spun and slammed the door shut.

"Your key is still out here," Jake called.

I tugged open the door, yanked the key out of the hole, and slammed it back closed, blushing all over again.

This time, I was definitely sure I heard him laughing as he went down the steps.

If he noticed that the accidental kiss was bothering me, he…well, he wasn't hiding that fact at all.

TWELVE

UPSIDE #12: THE ONLY AWKWARD KISSES THAT HAPPEN ARE ON TV. OR, YOU KNOW. WITH YOUR BOSS.

I hovered awkwardly outside the hotel. It was seven-thirty in the morning, and I'd only been able to sleep because I'd popped a couple of Benadryl pills to knock me out.

I'd kissed my boss.

Technically, it was an accident. Much like most of the things that had happened since we'd "met" last weekend.

I hadn't even told my best friends. If I said the words out loud, it made them real. I could almost go to work today and pretend it never happened if I never actually vocalized the fact I'd kissed Jacob.

Did it count, though? We didn't mean to do it. It was that awkward half-kiss you see in the movies where nobody meant to do anything but say goodbye and go.

How I'd gotten this far and not been run over was anybody's guess.

I took a deep breath and finally walked into the hotel. It was so quiet since it was still early, and that gave me a chance to wander to the front desk and the concierge desk to check on the staff there before heading back to my office.

I put the key in the door, but it was already unlocked. Frowning, I pulled the key back out of the keyhole and pushed open the door.

The room was empty.

I glanced around the office like the silence was deceiving me. It wasn't. There was nowhere for anyone to hide, and I even checked under the desk just to make sure. I quickly peeked behind me to make sure nobody had witnessed that moment of idiocy.

Seeing the coast was clear, I pushed the door shut behind me and quickly scurried to my side of the desk.

But that wasn't my chair.

I jerked my head to Jake's side.

That wasn't the ugly velvet chair.

They were the nice chairs from the store. The ones I declared were so comfortable I could feel an orgasm coming on.

Why were they in my office? And why were there boxes on the—

The delivery. From when I was dragged kicking and screaming shopping with Jake. All right, I was dragged whining and bitching, but they're practically the same thing where he's concerned.

It still remained as the shopping trip from hell, and it'd take another round of prom dress shopping to top it.

I wasn't doing that again. I didn't care if it was my daughter, my niece, or whoever else crawled out of someone's vagina. Twice was enough, thank you very much.

The bathroom door opened.

I screamed. My foot got caught on the fancy new bottom of the swirly, twisty desk chair, and I stumbled backward, my life flashing before my eyes in a cascade of two-second video highlights, right before I grabbed the shelf on the bookcase behind me.

The weak wood cracked.

The shelf shattered, I fell backward, hitting my tailbone on the very bottom shelf, and a paperback book bounced off the top of my head to the floor.

Just when I thought I was safe, a vanilla Yankee Candle slid off a top shelf, hit the back of my new chair, and smashed onto the floor.

"Ohhh," I moaned, rubbing the top of my head. And my back. How did I not twist my ankle on my travel down to the depths of Hell?

"What the…" Jake stopped in the doorway, his hand still clutching the doorknob. His gaze surveyed the damage my ass had created in the office.

Silence.

My butt hurt. My tailbone hurt. My hands hurt. And hell, everything hurt.

Mostly my pride.

Almost all my pride.

And my dignity.

And given the fact my skirt was halfway up to my hips…

I needed a big old rock to crawl under and come back out of in a few months.

"Now, spitfire," Jake started, his eyes finally landing on me. "I know you're Calamity Jane and capable of falling over thin air, but how the hell did you manage this?"

"Will you shut up and help me up? My ass hurts!"

He moved quickly across the room and not only lent a hand—he wrapped one of his strong arms around me and literally scooped me off the floor, only to deposit me into my apparently new office chair.

"This is quite something," he said.

I clutched my tailbone and pointed my finger at him. "You! Oooh."

"The hell did I do?"

"You hid in the bathroom?"

"I peed in the bathroom. I wasn't exactly undercover."

"You scared me!" I kicked my foot in his direction with the strength of an uncooked sausage. "You need a bell around your neck, so I know when you're coming!"

Jake didn't say a word. His eyes, though? Those lips, though? The roguish glint and the wolfish upturn told me everything I needed to know about what was going through his mind.

"Don't even—"

"A groan would be more appropriate, don't you think?"

"—think about it!" I grabbed a lime-green highlighter from my pot and threw it across the room at his head.

He ducked, batting it to the side with his hand. "Woah, woah! Calm down! I'd ask if you hit your head, but I know you're just this feisty."

"I am not feisty!"

Two gentle knocks sounded at the door.

"Come in," Jake said, ignoring my current predicament of my skirt still being halfway up to my hips.

Lillie edged her way in. She took one look at me and raised her eyebrows, meeting my eyes for a fleeting but serious moment before she turned her attention fully to Jake. "Mr. Creed, there's a Mr. Decaux on the phone for you. He says it's real urgent."

The contractor. I knew that name.

"Thank you, Lillie. Will you tell Mr. Decaux I'm in the middle of a meeting with my manager and I'll call him back at my earliest opportunity? As you can see, we need a clean-up."

Lillie's eyes swung from me holding my back with my hiked-up skirt to the broken shelf to Jake's mussed-up hair. She fought a smile. "Of course, sir."

"Oh, Jesus, no!" I shouted as she shut the door. "What did you say that for?"

Jake looked at the door then at me, blinking as if he genuinely had no idea what I was talking about. "What?"

Oh, God. He didn't.

"My skirt! The shelf!"

He didn't say a thing.

"Your hair looks like I've been running my nails through it in the heat of passion!"

"In a wild make-out session, you mean."

"Does it matter? Oooh!" I threw another highlighter at him. Orange, this time. If anyone was keeping count. "She thinks we've been getting it on when all that happened was you scaring the ever-loving shit out of me, so I wrecked half the place!"

He dropped his eyes to my feet. "Talking of...Those are high heels. Did you hurt yourself?"

"Only my ass and my pride!"

"After the boob thing, the bra thing, and the cobblestones, I didn't know you had much pride left where I was concerned. Oh—and don't forget the gin." He grinned.

The bastard.

"Now, you listen here." I stood up and pointed my finger at him. "All those things were accidental. They were not my fault. I'm a sucker for a dare, and that's why you know what my boobs look like."

"Not unfortunately."

"You are the one who showed up at my house unexpected and uninvited, and that's why you know what my bra looks like!"

"A very nice bra. Victoria's Secret?"

"The cobblestones last night were wet, and that was a freak accident."

"That had you landing in my arms."

"And the gin! Ohh, the gin. That's your fault for scaring the life out of me!"

"Like the shelf, right?" He grinned. A shit-eating, cocky as fuck grin that said he was playing along.

Unfortunately for my big mouth, I was on a roll.

"Like the shelf! And that kiss last night? Not my fault, either. Nope. You went for the cheek, and I went for the front door. That kiss was all your fault, buddy!"

I froze.

All the fresh air seemed to be sucked from the room.

My playful tantrum had turned into something more.

Something more real. Something that wasn't funny or brushed off with a bit of sarcastic banter.

Something I hadn't intended to bring up.

My grandma always said I had a big mouth and it'd get me in trouble one day...

Jake's eyes shone brightly, swirling with attraction and amusement, lust and frustration. "Did I go for the cheek?"

My mouth opened, and there were words in my mind, but nothing happened. I was forcing out air because there were no words.

There was nothing more than six feet between us, and he closed that distance in what seemed like seconds.

Then he was there. In front of me. Eyes blazing gray and lips pursed and stubble ready to be touched by my fingers.

My heart thundered.

I couldn't look at him, but I couldn't look away. Every second my eyes stayed trained on his was almost painful, from the goosebumps to the hairs to the way my stomach tightened whenever he got close.

He set me on fire.

He wasn't even touching me.

There were inches between us, but I could feel him anyway. I could feel how every exhale filled the air between us and how every inhale took away from it. How he gave and took away with each breath he took.

How he gave and took as he came one step closer.

Gave me butterflies.

Took any rationality.

Gave me wildness.

Took sensibility.

He reached for me. His fingertips ghosted along the side of my face, tickling across my temple until they reached my hair. He tucked the loose, wispy locks behind my ear, using the intimate touch to close the very final inches between us.

His breath.

I could feel it.

His heartbeat.

It beat hard enough that I could feel its vibrations on me.

His touch.

It electrified me.

"Oh, Mellie," he murmured, bringing his face closer to mine. His nose. His lips. The taste of his tongue. Always closer. "You think that was a kiss, spitfire? That wasn't a kiss. This is a kiss."

His fingers slipped into my hair. His lips found mine like he had a map from him to me, and my eyes fluttered shut at the pure ecstasy that spread through me at the simple yet intimate touch.

Slow, at first. Then more probing, but still not too forceful. That was how he kissed me. He kissed me like I was a treasure chest worth exploring. He kissed me like I was worth millions of hidden gold.

He kissed me like he'd never kiss another woman again, and I reveled in his touch.

One hand in my hair, fingers fisting the loose locks and tugging them against my scalp.

One hand circling my waist, tickling against my skin and digging in to hold me as close as possible.

Hands. Fingers. Hips. Chest. Lips. Tongue.

Soul-deep. I felt his kiss soul-deep, and it wound around my soul and latched onto a piece of it.

My hands slid up his chest and one cupped the side of his neck. I was against the wall now, my lower back still throbbing, but I barely cared. If it didn't feel as good as his tongue teasing mine into battle for dominance, I didn't care.

I could barely breathe through it. Nothing mattered other than the way he kissed me.

Like he meant it.

Which was ridiculous, but here I was, against the wall, kissing him like I meant it.

Hell.

Maybe I did.

Knock. Knock. Knock.

It cut through the kiss like a hot knife through butter. But he didn't jump away. He flattened his hands on the wall and turned his face in the direction of the door.

"Who is it?" Jake snapped.

"Lillie," she said. "It's Mr. Decaux on the phone for you again, Mr. Creed."

"Fucking hell," he said under his breath before he pushed off from the wall. "Co—"

I shook my head. His mouth was covered in my lipstick. Clearly, I hadn't bothered to wear anything long-lasting, today of all days. I motioned to my mouth, hoping he'd get the message.

"Hold on," he called.

I opened my drawer and pulled out a make-out wipe packet. Tearing a wipe from the packet, I raised my eyebrows to tell him to shut up. He obliged, and only looked at me strangely once when I wiped every last remnant of my makeup off his mouth.

"Bathroom," he whispered, shoving me in that direction.

I didn't argue. I went. My heart beating furiously and my entire body wanting more than just that kiss.

I shut the door behind me and leaned against it.

Holy. Shit.

What did I just do?

T H I R T E E N

Jacob

UPSIDE #13: THE ONLY BLONDE YOU WANT TO FUCK OVER A DESK IS ONE YOU SEE IN PORN. UNLESS MELANIE ROGERS KISSES YOU LIKE SHE'S DROWNING. THEN YOU FORGET THE PORN.

Motherfucker.

My cock throbbed like a teenage boy's. What the fuck did I do now? Lillie was on the other side of the door, and all I could think about was how Mellie gasped beneath my lips. All I could fucking think about was how she melded with my body and my touch and let my tongue battle hers.

How she'd let me pin her to a wall and kiss her until I couldn't breathe anymore. Until she couldn't breathe.

All I could think about was how the line had been there, and I'd crossed it.

Last night had been an accident. Sure—I'd thought about it. What it'd be like to kiss her and whether she'd taste like the Refreshers she drinks or the sugary sweetness of the powdered donuts she was so obsessed with.

I'd thought about it too much. But that didn't mean I wanted to act on it. Shit, no, that was a lie. I wanted to act on it.

I always had since the moment she turned around in the cellar and dropped the gin bottle.

I shouldn't act on it. It was wrong. We work together. She was my employee. I knew it was wrong, but for some fucking stupid reason, that just made me want her even more.

"Uh, Mr. Creed?" Lillie called.

I quickly sat on Mellie's side of the desk and adjusted my throbbing cock. "Come in."

She tentatively opened the door and held up the phone. "He's on hold. He keeps calling."

"Did you tell him I'd call him back?"

"Four times. He won't listen to me."

The bathroom door clicked open.

I hope she'd looked in the damn mirror...

Mellie stepped out, as perfectly put together as she had been before I'd given into temptation. Her hair was smoothed back, her lipstick reapplied, and any smudges had been wiped clean away.

"Pass it here." She held out her hand for the phone, and Lillie passed it over. Mellie pushed one button before raising it to her ear. "Hello, Mr. Decaux?"

Moments passed.

"No, this is Melanie Rogers, the manager of the hotel. I understand you're looking for Mr. Creed, but he's not available right now." She paused. "No, I can't make him available. Mr. Creed had to leave shortly after our meeting to handle some personal business... That's correct. He's not here, so I have to politely ask you to stop calling my hotel and commandeering my phone lines, or I'll call the police and report you for harassment... Mhmm... I'll be sure to pass that on for you when I see him next. Have a lovely day, Mr. Decaux." She hit a button on the phone, turned to Lillie, and handed it back. "Done. He won't be bothering you anymore." Then, she looked at me. "Call him tomorrow before we all lose our minds, okay?"

I quirked a brow. "Yes, boss."

She shot me a withering look. Whatever wildness had taken her over before was now gone. "I'm going to get some work done."

In other words, she was avoiding having to talk to me. "I'll clean up the mess you made, shall I, clumsy?"

"I'll ask Rosa to send one of the maids in. And I didn't make it—you made me make it. I told you that already." With that, she spun on her shiny black heels and stalked out of the office, her tight skirt drawing my attention down to her pert ass.

God damn. What was I doing?

———◦•◦———

"I don't see the problem." Sam put my boxes of take-out Chinese in front of me. "You're already over half of the most awkward part—seeing someone naked."

I shook my head. "She's my employee."

"And you've done a fucking awesome job of keeping that separate so far, haven't you?"

I flipped him the bird. Not only could neither of us cook, but we reverted to teenage boys whenever we were together. Our moms would be so proud.

"She's a great person to be around. She's easy to be around, to put it simply. It's easy to forget who she is," I admitted. "Until she fucking ignores me, then I remember again."

"So, let me get this straight." Sam wiped his mouth with the back of his hand. "You scared her, she almost burned the place down, she yelled, you kissed her, then she went out of her way to avoid you for the rest of the working day."

"She didn't burn the place down, but only because the candle wasn't lit. Otherwise, all bets are off."

"How can one adult woman be so clumsy and not have seriously hurt herself by now?"

"Believe me," I said. "I've been asking myself that question every day for the past week. "I've seen her in action, and she never gets injured."

"Now you've said it, she'll injure herself slicing a banana or something."

"That's definitely jinxed her." I sipped from my bottle of beer just as my phone buzzed. I picked it up and opened the message.

Mellie: *You never explained the new chairs.*

I snorted, almost coughing on my beer. I put the bottle down and replied.

Me: *You went off on a tangent and decided to ignore me after that.*

Mellie: *I wasn't ignoring you.*

Me: *Avoiding...ignoring...semantics.*

Mellie: *I had a lot of work to do and when I got back to the office you'd gone. Not my fault you left.*

Me: *You were avoiding me.*

Mellie: *I wasn't.*

Me: *You were.*

Mellie: *I wasn't.*

Me: *I'm not sorry I kissed you, spitfire. If you're fishing for an apology, you're not going to get one.*

She didn't reply straight away. I put my phone back down and, ignoring Sam's quizzical look, went back to my food. My cousin opened his mouth but was swiftly interrupted by the ringing of his own phone.

He pulled it from his pocket, looked at the screen, grinned at me, then headed for his room.

I shook my head, and my phone buzzed again.

Mellie: *I'm not sorry you kissed me, either.*

FOURTEEN

Mellie

UPSIDE #14: THE REMOTE CONTROL IS ALL MINE. BUT THAT ALSO MEANS MOVING TO GET IT, SOMETIMES...

"This is a mess," I said.

"So is this guy's submission. You'd think he'd let the cuts heal before taking the photo." Peyton turned her eleven-inch laptop around so we could see the screen.

I winced. I did not need to see anyone's penis this early in the morning. Or at all.

"Peyt. Seriously." Chloe grabbed the top of the screen and closed it down. "I'm trying to eat, and Mellie is in crisis."

"Mellie's always in crisis. It's in her DNA. If it weren't from this, it'll be from the papercut she got opening the donut bag."

I wanted to argue that, but...she was right.

The papercut really hurt, actually.

I groaned and leaned forward on the table, burying my face in my hands.

"Do you ever think we should work out more, considering the number of donuts we eat?" Peyton asked.

"Peyton," Chloe snapped. "We just did yoga, but that's not the point! Do you always have to be the bad cop?"

"Yes. You're the good cop. That's how this works. Someone needs to give tough love in this friendship."

I groaned again.

Peyton tugged at my hair. "Mellie, it doesn't matter. You know that. He's your boss."

I sat up and looked at her. "That's reassuring."

"Hush." She held a finger up to her lips. "It's just a kiss. One kiss. That's all. It's not like you can't come back from that. You just go in there tomorrow, put your foot down, and tell him this isn't happening. That it's unprofessional, it won't work, and it's completely ridiculous to think that it might happen."

I blinked at her. "I'm not that great at putting my foot down."

"Are you kidding?" Chloe laughed. "Do you not remember when Rex Tyson tried to call you out for not putting out in senior year? You literally threw a test tube at his head and told him if he'd had a little thing called respect, you might have screwed him that weekend."

"That's not putting my foot down."

"Oh! I remember that!" Peyton clapped her hands, almost dropping her pink donut in the process. "Right after, when he apologized, you told him in no uncertain terms the only thing that would be putting out that weekend was his hand when he thought about you in the shower."

"Oh," I muttered. "I remember that."

"Just do it again," Chloe continued. "You know as well as we do that work relationships don't work."

Peyton rolled her eyes. "From the girl in love with her business partner."

"I am not in love with your brother!" Chloe smacked her hand against the table.

"And I'm a virgin," I said immediately. "Work relationships don't work. You're right. I mean, he's handsome and a really great guy, but he's my boss. That's just asking for trouble."

My best friends both nodded in agreement.

Right. So I had to lay out the law. I'd done it once already, hadn't I? No talking about my boobs.

I could do it again.

No kissing.

Except I didn't regret it.

I didn't regret kissing him when he'd grabbed hold of me. How could I? It'd been the most electric kiss I'd ever had, and I'd been unable to think of anything else since. I'd been the one to put my foot in it about the kiss the night before.

What was I expecting?

An apology?

No. I knew I wouldn't get one. You didn't kiss a girl the way he kissed me and apologize for it, because you didn't kiss anyone like that if you didn't mean it.

And if you apologized for something you meant, you were an idiot.

Especially when a kiss felt the way it had.

But I could put my foot down. If he kissed me again, I knew there'd be no coming back from it. There'd be no way I'd be able to work with him.

I had to tell him that was it. That was the first and only kiss we could share. It didn't matter that I didn't regret it, something he knew, it just mattered that it never happened again.

Nothing good ever came from kissing your boss.

Not once, not twice, not ever.

"Put my foot down. I can do that." I nodded.

Chloe's phone rang, and she got up from the table to grab it from it sofa. She missed the call by seconds, but she froze, leaning toward the window on one leg. "Uhh…Does Jacob drive an Audi?"

I jerked my head up. "Yes."

"Does he have dark hair and wear a white shirt like hookers wear thongs?"

Peyton choked on her coffee.

"Um...yes," I answered.

"Does he have an ass like a giant, ripe peach?" Chloe continued, craning her neck.

I rubbed my nose. "I mean, I haven't looked, but..."

"Filthy liar," Peyton snapped.

"Yes! He has an ass like a giant, ripe peach! My God!"

Chloe grimaced, turning around to face me. "Does he show up randomly at your house?"

I jumped out of my chair. "Shut up! No!"

She pointed at the door. "There's a hot guy who just pulled up in an Audi unexpectedly with dark hair, who wears a white shirt the way hookers wear thongs and has an ass like a giant, ripe peach."

Three loud knocks sounded at my door.

"Oh God!" I moaned, clutching at my stomach. "I have to hide. Can you stall him?"

Peyton grinned. A shit-eating warning grin.

"Actually, no, never mind," I whispered harshly. "Peyton, you go out the back, I'll hide, and Chloe can get rid of him!"

Peyt shook her head. "Not a chance. Who is it?" she added, shouting the last three words.

I clapped my hands over my mouth. Not only was this not a good time because I was still freaking out over the kissing, but we'd just finished a yoga DVD, and I was still sweaty and gross. Not to mention I was pretty sure I'd pulled a muscle.

And the powder. I was covered in donut sugar, okay?

"Uh... It's Jake," came the reply through the door.

Peyt waggled her eyebrows. "Jake, eh?"

I glared at her then stuck my middle finger up in her direction. "I hate you."

The door hinges creaked, and the next thing I knew, Chloe was standing in the door frame. "Hi!" she said in an upbeat tone. "I'm Chloe." She shoved her hand at him.

"Jake," he replied slowly, taking her hand. "Is Mellie here?"

"She's here, but she might be hiding."

Peyton burst out laughing. My cheeks flamed red, and I stormed across the room and tugged her away from the door.

"Hi. Excuse her. She didn't take her meds this morning," I said.

Chloe poked my cheek. "Hello, Mommy. Did you bring me my cookies?"

Peyton, still laughing, stood up. "Okay, Chlo, drop it. Let's go. We have work to do."

I spun around as she slipped her laptop into her purse. "And you need to leave to do that? You literally just showed us a penis photo."

"Your house doesn't have the right feng shui."

"You've never looked up feng shui!"

She pointed a finger in my direction. "You don't know my life!"

Jake blinked between the three of us.

Chloe grabbed hold of her purse and then Peyton's arm. "We're going. Call us later, okay?"

Jake moved out of the way while Chloe dragged Peyton out of my house.

"And don't forget to put your foot down on the kissing thing!" Peyton shouted, eyes sparkling. The last I saw of her was a large, mischievous grin right before Jake shoved the door shut on her.

I collapsed back onto my sofa and buried my face in my hands. "Thank you for that."

"Me or her?" he asked.

"Her sarcastically, you genuinely." I dropped my hand. "This isn't awkward at all."

Jake grinned, half-stuffing his hands into his pockets. "If it helps, I was here to talk about the 'kissing thing.'"

"Not really." I swung my legs up onto the sofa and tucked my feet close to my ass. "I was hoping to not talk about it, but my friends are so helpful."

"If they know, you've been talking about it."

"I'm not going to sit here and feed your ego." I jumped up off the sofa and walked to the kitchen. "I don't want to discuss this at all." I pulled a donut from the bag and bit into it without looking.

Sprinkles.

Bah.

I darted to the trash can and spat my mouthful into it, followed swiftly by the rest of the donut.

"Did I just see you spit out donut?" Jake joined me in the kitchen, eyebrows raised.

I looked down. "I hate sprinkles," I said quietly. "It's like rolling sugar in my mouth."

"You hate sprinkles?"

"I hate sprinkles," I repeated. Then pulled the last sugar donut out of the bag, leaving the two sprinkled ones left.

My phone rang. Chloe's name flashed on the screen, and I hit "answer" then "speaker." "What?" I demanded.

"I left my donuts," Peyton whined. "Can you open the door and give them to me?"

"Sure. Two seconds." I hung up, grabbed the bag, and walked toward my living room window. Jake's eyebrows shot up, and Chloe's eyes widened when I opened the door, brandishing the brown bag.

"Peyton!" Chloe shouted.

"Your stupid bakery put my donuts in with your stupid sprinkles! I ate one and threw it out!" I called out of the window. "And for the stunt you just pulled, Peyton Austin—"

"Don't throw my donuts!" she hollered, jumping down my steps.

"—you can catch them!"

Sadly, she caught them. But I pointed two fingers at my eyes, then at her. Her response was to make the universal blow-job sign with her hand and her tongue.

I was told I'd grow up.

Someone was wrong.

I tugged the window shut and turned around. Jake was now perched on the edge of my kitchen table. His lips were curved in amusement and his arms were folded across his chest like he was watching a stand-up comedy show live.

He probably was, in all honesty.

"So. This isn't awkward at all," I said, wringing my fingers.

He quirked a brow. "I actually came here to talk about what happened, but it seems like you've already decided what you need to say."

I dropped my hands and put them on my hips. "Yes. That, um, the kiss. It can't happen again."

He hooked his thumbs in his belt loops.

"We work together. It's completely inappropriate."

He tilted his head to the side, lips twitching.

"You're my boss. It was a mistake. It can't happen again."

"All right," Jake said.

All right.

Just all right.

"All right?" I repeated. "You didn't come here to tell me that."

"How do you know what I came here to say?"

"I don't, but I'd bet good money it wasn't to tell me it can't happen again." I twirled a loose thread from the hem of my shirt around my finger lightly.

He blew out a long breath. "You're right. It wasn't. But that doesn't change the fact that you're correct. It can't happen again."

I blinked at him. I don't know what I was expecting him to say, but it wasn't that.

"Don't look so shocked, spitfire. You're the one who just said it."

"I wasn't expecting you to agree with me."

"That's obvious by the look on your face." He pushed off the table and walked toward me. "Look. It happened. I'm not going to stand in front of you and deny that I'm extremely attracted to you. Without even considering the fact I've seen your boobs."

I grimaced.

He tried not to laugh. "But, you're right. We work together. It's bad enough working with you now when you argue with me over desk space and the whole toilet seat thing."

"Still not forgiven for that, by the way."

"See? That's my point. If this is bad, I can't imagine how intolerable you'd be if I did something like made your coffee wrong or left the toilet seat up at your house as well as at work."

The image of me cussing him out because of the toilet seat while he made coffee, shirtless in my kitchen, flashed through my mind.

I beat it away. There was no place for it. Not in my mind and not in reality.

Tell that to the butterfly making me feel sick in my stomach.

"And the money I'd have to spend to baby-proof this house so you don't hurt yourself?" He shook his head. "Why has nobody done that, actually?"

"Because I pretty much only hurt myself when you're around. There's a link. You called me, I stubbed my toe. You on my sofa, I kicked the table. You in the street, I trip on a cobblestone. You scare me, I take out half the office. You see the pattern here?"

"Yes. You're determined to fall at my feet." He grinned.

I stared at him, reaffirming my stance with my hands on my hips. "In your dreams. We've spent way too much time together outside of work, and that's why we kissed. It's that simple. We know each other more than the average boss and employee."

"True. And we can change that."

"He says while standing in my house."

He held up his hands. "I came here to clear the air before work tomorrow, and that's what we're doing."

I nodded once. "Right. So, we're clear. Just work. We're not friends, just boss and employee. And there will be no more discussing my boobs. And we definitely can't kiss again."

"Boss and employee, not friends. No more boob-talk. And we can't kiss again," he summarized.

"Perfect."

Our eyes met, and the silence that stretched between us was heavy. Thick and uncomfortable, almost as if it were full of lies.

"Well, I hope like hell you have more resolve than I do," Jake said softly, breaking the silence while keeping his gaze locked on mine.

"Wh—why is that?" I was afraid to ask—to hear the answer.

I was right to be.

He reached out, and his fingertips grazed across my temple as he tucked my hair behind my ear. "Just because I *can't* kiss you again, doesn't mean I *won't*."

I swallowed, stepping back. "That's not how it works."

"I know." Jake put his hands in his pockets, briefly glancing away before his gaze collided with mine once again. "Which is why I hope you're a stronger person than I am."

He turned on those last words and walked toward my front door. He put his hand on the handle, and I said, "I thought you weren't sorry."

He looked over his shoulder, gray eyes shining as they found mine. "I'm not. Let's make it clear, Mellie." He dropped the handle and walked straight back to me, stopping right in front of me so I had to crane my neck back to look at him. "I'm not sorry. I could kiss you right now, and apart from kicking myself for breaking the one rule I just made, I still wouldn't be sorry." He cupped my chin, tilting his face down to mine. "Wanting to kiss you and refusing to, doesn't make me regret the fact I did. It makes me regret the fact I had to be the person who bought your hotel, but at the same time, if I hadn't bought it, I would never know who the crazy, attitude-filled, beautiful blonde who flashed me was."

"I'm confused," I said quietly.

"Yeah. Try being in my head." He half-smiled. "Don't confuse me doing the right thing with not wanting you."

I tried to reply to that, but I couldn't. Which was a good thing, because this time, when Jake went to the door, I wasn't stupid enough to speak and stop him. I stood in silence and watched him leave.

The click of the door as it shut echoed through my silent house.

I blew out a long breath and fell back onto my sofa. My heart was pounding wildly, and I didn't even know just how hard until now. Now he was gone, and I was alone, and I had to process what he'd just said.

None of it made sense.

I'd done what I'd had to do. I'd put my foot down. Made it clear where I stood.

He'd tried to do the same, but instead of clearing the air, I was afraid he'd started a storm.

Because if he was expecting me to be the stronger person...he was wrong.

If he kissed me again—today, tomorrow, a month from now, there wasn't a chance in hell I'd be pushing him away.

And that meant I was in trouble.

It also meant I needed to grow a pair, but I'd think about that tomorrow when my heart wasn't trying to kill me and my legs weren't screaming in pain.

Instead, I planned to run a hot bath and do what all women did when men said dumb shit: overthink it until I'd successfully solved why penguins can't fly.

FIFTEEN

UPSIDE #15: THE ONLY THING YOU HAVE TO OVERTHINK IS WHETHER OR NOT YOU CAN GET AWAY WITH THAT DRESS. THE KEY: WHETHER OR NOT YOUR MOTHER WILL TAKE ONE LOOK AT YOU AND ASK YOU IF YOU'RE PREGNANT.

Every time someone walked past my office, I flinched. I kept the door ajar so I wouldn't be shocked when Jake arrived, but ever since he'd left my house and I'd had my bath—in which I'd thought so much I solved world hunger and the homeless crisis, thank you very much—I'd been on edge thinking about what would happen when I saw him.

If we were now boss and employee, did I have to call him Mr. Creed? Would he now call me Melanie all the time? Would it be awkward when we sat across the desk from each other?

Oh, Jesus. Of course, it would be awkward. I knew what he tasted like, for the love of God. I couldn't stop thinking about how he kissed.

If I thought my crush was a schoolgirl one before, I'd obviously forgotten what it was like to be in high school.

What the hell was I doing? The only way this would be comfortable was if we didn't work together. But equally, I refused to leave my job because of a man.

I had to grow a pair. I had to stop thinking of him the way I was.

If only it were that easy. He was as close to perfect as a guy could get. Which meant he either had a very small penis or a problem with ingrown toenails. Maybe he couldn't read, or he had an uncomfortably close relationship with a female relative.

There had to be something wrong with him. Nobody, and I mean nobody, could kiss that well, be that good looking, and be as much of a gentleman as Jacob Creed was, without having something wrong with them.

It was that simple.

Like me. I was arguably rather pretty. I was successful, I could cook, and I was a bit of a green-thumbed girl. It was a shame about my clumsiness, or Jane Austen would have married me off by now.

My mother would have married me off by now if I hadn't smashed Davy Boudreau's mama's favorite vase at a party. In my defense, I warned her I couldn't dance.

I also warned my mother I wasn't cut out for the high-society in this city, which she really should have known when the man hired to teach me to dance quit because I kept stepping on his toes.

It was a miracle I could cook without burning so much as my finger, really.

I unscrewed the cap on my water bottle and looked out of the window as I took a drink. There was a stack of paperwork sitting on my desk, but all I could think about was what was wrong with Jacob Creed.

That charming smile had to hide something. The devil wore many disguises, according to my grandma.

Then again, she also thought chickens were the devil's minions, so her logic was questionable.

"Hey."

I spat out half my water and choked on the other half.

Jake sighed. "You're right. I'm the common denominator here. Try not to choke to death on my account, yeah?"

I thumped my chest and put the bottle on the desk. Waving my hand to tell him to shut up, I managed to get rid of the horrible tickle in my throat.

"You didn't hear me coming? Lillie stopped me to warn me you've been like a nervous beetle all morning." Jake pushed the door fully shut and put a white paper bag on the desk. "What's wrong with you?"

"I was thinking about my grandma and her feelings about chickens," I said slowly, reaching for the cap to put back on the bottle. "Don't ask."

He raised one eyebrow, a la The Rock style. Questioning, confused expression and everything. "Part of me tells me I shouldn't, but honestly, I do have questions."

I waved him away. "It's too early for that." I turned back to the mound of paperwork when a couple of envelopes caught my eye. "Oh, by the way," I said, reaching for them. "You had mail this morning."

"Thanks." He took them from me and glanced at them. "I'll open those in a minute. I didn't eat yet." He opened the white bag and pulled out several smaller bags with the top folded over. "Here. This one is yours."

Tentatively, I took the bag from him. "Aren't we supposed to be not-friends?"

"Yes." He picked up the other bags and held them up. "I'm being a good boss and bought donuts and pastries for everyone. I'm going to put them in the staff area now."

I blinked at him as he left, leaving one single bag on the desk behind him.

I couldn't say for sure, but that sounded an awful lot like someone was bending the rules.

And God, the donuts were still hot.

I pulled one out and bit into it. It was an explosion of sugar and gooey goodness on my tongue—and on the paperwork I was supposed to be working on. Rolling my eyes at my own stupidity, but also thanking my lucky stars that was the most mess I'd made today, I wiped it off onto the floor and set the half-eaten donut on top of the paper bag.

Well, it was the most mess I'd made if you didn't count the water, and I didn't. It was water. If water was a mess, the Earth needed a real damn good clean up.

Damn. I could have done with that line as a kid.

I managed to get through several bits of the paperwork—and the donut—before Jake made it back to the office. If I was being honest, he looked pretty damn smug and proud of himself.

He grinned ear-to-ear, and there was something overly endearing about the way his eyes sparkled. Hell, he was even whistling.

Why was he whistling?

"Why are you whistling? And can you please stop?" I pressed against my ear to get rid of the lingering ring from the awful noise.

Jake grinned at me. "I'm in a good mood, and I happen to whistle a lot when that happens."

"You either just bribed your staff with baked goods or you gave them them so you could get around buying me donuts."

"Someone thinks a lot of herself this morning."

"Someone sees through your bullshit."

He snorted and sat down. "I can neither deny or confirm your accusations."

"You're so full of shit. It's not even been twenty-four hours, and you're already breaking all your rules."

He leaned back in his hair, a smug smile on his face. "And you were supposed to be the strong one, but you're covered in powdered sugar."

"Look." I rested my elbow on the table and pointed my pen at him. "If you hand me donuts, I'm going to eat them.

That means I'm weak where donuts are concerned, not where you are."

"You once told me donuts are the way to your heart."

"That has nothing to do with this."

His eyes sparkled. "I literally just bought my way into your heart."

I stared at him. "That's literally the worst line I've ever heard in my life, and my friends run hook-up and dating websites. Chloe has a page of bad pick-up lines on her website."

Jake winced, rubbing his hand down his face. "Yeah, it sounded a lot smoother in my head. Can we try that again?"

"No!" I laughed, slamming my pen down. "My God. You're a weak, weak man! We have a deal, and no matter what you say, we're sticking to it. No kissing, no being friends, and..." I glanced at the donut bag.

"You were about to tell me not to buy donuts again, weren't you?"

"I believe I already asked that."

"I can stop if you really want me to."

"Woah, woah. Let's not be too hasty in making that decision now." I paused. "You really should continue in the interest of boss-employee relations."

He raised his eyebrows, lips pulling into a sexy little smirk like the one I saw the very first night we met. "There are a lot of things we can do in the interest of boss-employee relations, but since almost all of them start with kissing, you've vetoed that."

"You did a veto, too!"

"I was being a gentleman."

"Oh, so our conversation yesterday was a waste of both our time? Well, thank God for that. I love meaningless conversations with people who don't listen to me."

"Hey, spitfire. I listened to you. Every word."

I glared at him. "You forgot the part where we're not friends and not kissing!" I finished on a hiss.

Jake paused, his gaze flitting across my face before he glanced down at where I'd picked the pen back up and was squeezing it tightly. "I don't know," he started. "This is an awful lot like not friends, and definitely not even close to kissing."

I threw my pen at him.

He was quick. His hand shot out, and he snatched the pen from the air before it could make contact with him. "Your aim is dreadful."

"Good. It's probably friends with your self-control!"

He looked like he was going to say something, but instead, he burst out laughing. I glared at him while he laughed at me, seemingly not caring he was winding me up more and more by the minute.

I crossed my arms over my chest and kept staring at him. Unfortunately for me, the longer I did it, the harder he laughed.

"You're right," he finally said. "My self-control is dreadful. And it doesn't help when your top button is undone."

I jerked my head down, and damn it, he was right. The stupid thing must have worked its way free while I was working. I quickly did it back up and then placed my hand there just in case.

"That's not an excuse for your weakness," I told him. "You haven't even tried."

"I don't want to try."

"So, you're going to spend our working hours trying to seduce me while I have to resist you? Won't that be bad for your ego?"

His eyebrows raised again. "Who said it was limited to just our working hours?"

I sat back and flicking my pen against the desk, said, "I don't know if you're messing with me or if you're serious. Or if you're just testing me to see if I'll give in or not."

"Well, if you give in, I'm gonna give in, so you can nix that last one."

"Oh, well, that narrows it down," I said dryly. "Thanks for the help."

"You're welcome." He grinned. The same grin that always sent butterflies through me. This time, it sent a shiver down my spine. "Look, the reason I buy you donuts is because if food is the way to your heart, I'm screwed. I can't cook."

I stilled.

Oh, my God.

That was it.

"Why are you looking at me like I just kicked your puppy?" Jake asked.

I met his gaze. "You can't cook?"

"I can't cook," he replied slowly, fidgeting. "Why?"

"Oh my God. That's what's wrong with you."

He blinked at me, confusion clouding his eyes. "I'm so confused."

I clapped my hand over my mouth. I wasn't supposed to say that out loud. That thought was supposed to stay firmly inside my head.

Oh no.

"The fact I can't cook means there's something wrong with me?"

I met his eyes. Thankfully, he was halfway between confusion and all-out amusement. "I, um, never mind. Oh, look at that. It's my lunch break."

"It's ten-thirty."

"Brunch break! Same thing!" I got up and grabbed my purse.

The single flaw in my plan was that he was between me and the door.

Fine. Not the single plan, but the major one.

Jake stood, sending the chair flying back to the wall, and blocked my path to the door. "Tell me what you mean."

I mimed zipping my lips.

"Mellie."

I shook my head, clutching my purse to my stomach to put a barrier stronger than thin air between us.

"Melanie..." His voice took on a rougher, darker edge, and his eyes hardened, too. But not in a scary way. A weirdly sexy way.

I swallowed and took a step back. "I can take my brunch at lunch."

He grabbed me before I had a chance to escape back around to my side of the desk. In one swift movement, he snatched my purse from me, throwing it onto his chair, then spun me so my ass bumped into the desk.

Leaning forward, he planted his hands on either side of me on the desk.

I was trapped.

We both knew it.

And so did the boom-boom-boom beat of my heart as it went wild.

"Tell me what you mean by what you said," he said in a low voice, his face only inches from mine.

Well, I'd fucked up this much, so what was a little more honesty?

"I, um..." I reached up and pushed my hair from my face before I clasped my hands against my lower stomach. Making sure not to look him in the eye, I picked a spot on the wall behind him and said, "I was thinking earlier that something had to be wrong with you, that's all."

"Why?"

"Because, um, well..." *Spit it out, woman, God.* "Don't take this the wrong way, but—"

"How can I not take this the wrong way?"

"You're not letting me finish!"

He looked at me flatly. "Spitfire, you haven't even started explaining yet."

The man...had a point.

Damn it.

I hated it when that happened.

"Okay, fine." I huffed out a breath and retrained my gaze on that spot on the wall. "It works like this. You're handsome—"

"Am I, now?"

"—You're successful."

"Working on it."

"And you're incredibly humble," I added dryly, snapping my gaze to him. "Shut up and let me finish."

His lips tugged to the side. "Now, she looks at me. Go again. From the top. I'm enjoying this."

I licked my lips, bit back a smartass retort, and started again. "You're handsome. You're successful. You're a gentleman. And as far as kissing goes, you're not too bad at it. So, there had to be something wrong with you, and now I know. You can't cook. That's your negative."

He stared at me for a moment. "All I hear from that is that you've been thinking about me when I'm not around."

I opened my mouth.

Closed it.

Opened it.

Closed it.

Did anyone need help finding Nemo? I was apparently a new breed of fish with this mouth.

"You're not denying it." He grinned.

"I literally just admitted I was," I finally managed to get out. "But, there you go. There's your explanation. Can you let me go now, please?"

He put one finger against my lips but quickly returned his hand to the desk so I couldn't move. "Is not being able to cook a bad thing? Can you cook?"

"Of course, I can cook. I'm not carrying an extra ten pounds on my ass from starving, am I?" I rolled my eyes. "How do you eat if you can't cook?"

"Take-out."

"You live off take-out?"

"If you want to be judgmental, the reason you have an extra ten pounds on your ass is because your daily breakfast is donuts."

"Why you—" I stopped. This was another one of those situations where you couldn't argue with the truth. "I hate it when you're right."

He blinked in shock. "Holy shit. I thought you'd go right for the balls for that asshole comment."

I shrugged a shoulder. "It's true. Although the yoga probably balances it out at this point." At least, that's what I was telling myself. "I can't believe you live off take-out. Or that you're still trapping me against this desk."

"You're lucky that trapping you is all I'm doing, spitfire." A mischievous glint sparked in his eyes. "And I don't live off take-out. Only mostly. Sometimes, I'm a real adult who eats in restaurants."

"Or you could learn to cook."

"I make mean scrambled eggs."

"My eight-year-old cousin can make scrambled eggs." I raised my eyebrows. "You're not convincing me, Jake."

He sighed, dropping his head to the side. "Then, teach me."

"Oh no. No. I'm not falling for this." I jabbed him in the shoulder. "You're doing everything you can to break the rules we set—"

"You're doing a stellar job of following them right now."

"—And I'm not falling for your shit. Let me go."

His eyes shone with mirth, the laughter practically dancing in his gaze. "I'll let you go if you teach me how to cook."

"I'm not falling for this!"

He shrugged a shoulder, taking a step back until he was more comfortable. "Then, I guess we'll just stay here all day long, even if someone needs to come in here. That'll be some real awkward explaining…"

I crossed my arms. "I'm not doing it. You told me I had to be the one who'd resist, so that's what I'm doing. Resisting."

"All right. You sit there against the desk. Resisting." He moved his face an inch closer to mine. "And I'll stand here thinking about how many times I'd have to kiss your neck to make you turn and bend over it. Fair?"

No. That wasn't fair. That was playing dirty, and he knew it.

I clenched my thighs together. "More times than you'd be able to before I punched you right in the dick," I snapped.

"Since we'll be here a while, I should get started." His eyes flashed almost in a challenge, but...

He wouldn't, would he?

He wouldn't actually—

His lips brushed the base of my neck, just above where it curved down to my collarbone. A jolt of pleasure went skittering across my skin, and I inhaled sharply.

He smiled against my skin, then kissed me again.

"Fine!" I shoved him away from me and managed to actually break away from him. "Fine!" I dragged my hand through my hair and took a deep breath. "I will teach you to cook if you never do that again!"

Because goddamn it, he'd kissed my neck twice and my vagina was clenching in desire like it was Kegel time.

The smile that covered his face was triumphant and sexy and a little bit cocky. "Tonight."

I hesitated.

"I'll do it again," he warned.

I scooted back. "I hate you."

He smirked.

"Tonight," I agreed. "Six o'clock at my house. And it's nothing more than to get you off my back, do you understand?"

"Perfectly."

I shuffled back around to my side of the desk and sat down. "Now, go away and let me finish my work. Pain in the ass," I finished on a mutter.

"This is my office, too."

"Goddamn it."

SIXTEEN

UPSIDE #16: COOKING FOR ONE IS EASY. IT'S WHEN YOU HAVE TO MAKE PASTA FOR TWO PEOPLE THAT YOU REALIZE YOU HAVE THE COOKING SKILLS TO FEED A SMALL ARMY...AND HAVE LEFTOVERS.

"You didn't stir it, did you?"

Jake looked at the now-burned pasta stuck to the bottom and sides of the pan. "I stirred it. Once."

"How long ago did you stir it?"

He made an awkward face, bearing his perfectly straight teeth in such a way that he looked like the grimacing emoji.

I patted his arm and took the pan away from him. "It's a good thing you're pretty." I put the pan in the sink and mentally patted myself on the back for deciding that he needed a test run.

Good thing pasta was cheap.

I got a clean pan from the rack hanging inside the cupboard and passed it to him. "Fill it up with water and boil it. Do you think you can manage that without ruining something?"

"How can the clumsiest person in the world cook as smoothly as you can?" he grumbled, filling the pan.

"I've had a lot of practice."

"As opposed to the limited amount of practice at being a human being."

I poked my tongue out at him behind his back. "At least I can cook pasta, arguably the easiest thing in the world to do."

"I'm culinary-challenged, just like you're life-challenged."

"But I'll never starve." I handed him the salt. "Put a little of that into the water. It helps to stop the pasta sticking."

"You couldn't have told me that a minute ago?" Jake tipped the salt container and—

"I said a little bit, Jake! Why don't you just run to the coast and get me a pan full of seawater?"

He stopped, tipped the container upright, and looked at the foggy mess that would make the Gulf of Mexico cry with saltiness. "Well, shit."

"Move out of the way." I nudged—shoved—him out of my way, grabbed the pan and emptied it, then rinsed it out before going through filling it for the third time. I put the salt in my hand before adding two pinches and washing my palm off.

"Oh, well if you'd told me to do that..."

"You'd have still done it wrong." I rolled my eyes. "Do you think you can dice the chicken, or should I do it just in case?"

He stared at the knife on the board. "Honestly, everything in me says you aren't to be trusted with that knife."

Emotionless, I said, "Why? Because you're within stabbing distance?"

"I was going to say because you'd cut yourself, but now you're definitely right." He picked up the knife, then knocked on my head. "Hello? Satan? Are you in there?"

Despite myself, I laughed, batting his hand away. "Shut up. Dice it, but not too big, and not too small."

"Has anyone ever told you you're an excellent teacher? Your ability to give instructions is out of this world."

"There are other knives in this kitchen I can stab you with, Jake."

He peered back at me over his shoulder. "You look pretty today."

"I'm wearing yoga pants, a shirt with a sauce stain on it, and I think my socks have a hole in them. Try again, Romeo." I paused. "In fact, don't. You're not supposed to even be here, let alone compliment me."

"A boss can't be nice to his employee?" He put on a look of faux-shock.

I pulled the mushrooms from the fridge and hit him with a hard look. "Not when the only reason the boss is in the employee's house is because he crossed a line."

He inclined his head in acknowledgment and cut the chicken breast in half. "And then, you let me over the line."

"We aren't talking about this anymore. Shut up and cut the chicken."

"Should you be talking to your boss like that?"

I slammed the mushroom packet on the side. "When you're in my kitchen, there's only one boss, and I'm it. Is that clear?"

"Yes, ma'am."

"Call me ma'am again, and I will slice you like a tomato."

He fought a laugh just long enough for me to narrow my eyes and convey with my gaze that I was deadly serious. He quickly stopped laughing and went straight back to cutting the chicken and throwing the diced cubes into the pot.

I turned away, biting my lip to hide my smile, and reached for the pasta. Luckily for me, I'd bought two packets on impulse.

Clearly, my spidey-senses had shown up today.

I put the pasta in the now-boiling pan and threw a splash of oil in with the chicken. Miraculously, Jake managed to make it through cutting it all up without screwing it all up or cutting himself.

"Now what?" he asked.

"Now, you clean the board, so nobody gets food poisoning." I slid it off the counter and over to the sink. He followed me, watching as I ran the water until it was hot and rinsed the board off with some soap. "You do the knife and yourself, and I'll dry this."

"Yes, boss."

Cocky bastard.

I dried the board, then grabbed a new knife and sliced the onion in two, making sure to cut off the end. "Are you done?" I asked Jake.

"Yep." He came back over, wiping his hands on a towel. "What's next?"

"Slice the onion. I'll do the first half. Watch this." I peeled the layers of skin off the onion, checked the top layer of it, then set it down on the board. "Dice it like this," I said, making the first cut into the onion.

"How?" He moved closer.

"Pay attention."

He came even closer. He was all in my personal space, consuming every last bit of the air around me and filling it with his presence. My left arm brushed against his body every time I sliced, and I swallowed hard as the warmth from him seemed to radiate onto me.

"Ah. I see." He leaned right against the side of the counter. "Seems simple enough."

I turned the onion and diced the other way. My eyes were barely stinging, so either this onion was weak, or the general sensation of being around Jacob Creed was way more overwhelming than onion.

Probably not the best compliment I'd ever paid anyone. I'd keep that gem to myself.

"Then you just…scoop it up…" I said, doing just that. "And throw it in the pot with the chicken." I blinked and stepped back, clasping my hands together. My eyes flitted from meeting his gaze to the onion until I said, "You do the other half."

"I'll try." He picked up the other half of the onion, and with an almost endearing uncertainty, peeled off the first two layers of skin. "That enough?"

I peered over. "One more. The last one can be tricky. You have to get your nail under it a little."

He did as I said, frowning as he peeled off the last, pesky layer. "Now?"

"Now cut." It was almost cute I was teaching a basically thirty-year-old man how to slice an onion...and watching him do it wrong.

God help me.

"No, no. You don't slice across first. You slice into the onion." I used my finger to show him the proper direction. "You have to hold the layers together, but not cut all the way into it."

"Uhh..."

"Oh, Jesus Christ." I took the knife, and beckoning him to stay still, did two cuts to show him. "There. See? The onion is still together, but it'll dice easier when you cut across it."

"Like this?" He covered my hand with his and forced it into the onion correctly.

"Yes," I managed to get out.

"Uh-huh." He did it again, this time moving his body so he was almost completely behind me, his solid chest pressing against my back.

My ass was pretty much tucked against his groin, and I swallowed hard, willing my body not to react the way I knew it so easily could.

"Is this right?" he asked, slicing into it perfectly.

"Perfect," I eked out.

Tingles ran up and down my arm.

"Now...the other way." My throat was dry.

His arm muscles flexed against me when he twisted the onion and moved to cut it. My hand was still on the knife, trapped beneath his, and every time he exhaled, his breath fluttered my hair.

He sliced it perfectly.

It hit me.

He'd played me, and I'd fallen for it. I'd played right into his hands, getting in this position and so easily allowing him to basically wrap his body around mine.

"Is that done?" he said in a low voice, his mouth right by my ear.

I nodded. My heart thundered in my chest, skipping a beat when he used my hands to scoop up the onion and drop it into the pot.

Never. Never had I ever thought that cutting an onion could be sexy.

"Now what?" he asked, lips still in the same spot, except this time, they almost brushed against my earlobe.

"Mushrooms," I whispered. "And the burner needs turning on."

He leaned over the stove and turned on the burner that had the pot on it before reaching for the mushrooms and opening the packet. "How many?"

"Five. Maybe six."

"How do you cut them?"

I swallowed. "Slices."

"Show me."

I should have said no. I should have told him that if he didn't know how to slice mushrooms at his age, then he had no chance of being able to cook anything successfully.

But, I didn't. The pressure of his body against mine was too sweet. The way his breath tickled my hair and skin was too warm—it felt too good, all the time.

The way his fingers curled around mine on the knife handle sent too many shivers through me.

Yet, I couldn't change it. I couldn't say no and push him away and make it stop.

So, I sliced the mushroom, and when I grabbed the second, he took hold of the knife.

My chest was tight. My lungs wanted more air, but I had to fight it. There was no way I was going to make it even more obvious to him that I was going crazy inside. That he was sending my body into a tailspin of lust and desire that reverberated through every vein, mixing with a shot of adrenaline into a heady mix that defied logic.

He only released me to stir the chicken and pasta, something I'd forgotten about.

How could I remember how not to burn things when I was burning up myself?

How could I cook that, when the only thing that was cooking was my own damn insanity?

He'd got what he wanted, and right now, he was winning the battle, but my God—he would not win the war.

He could think he would, but I wasn't going to kiss him.

Not tonight.

Not ever again.

I didn't care how much I wanted to. I didn't care how hard my heart beat around him or how many times I had to clench my legs together because the ache in my clit was unbearably uncomfortable.

I didn't care.

Not one bit.

He turned his face into my hair. "Is that everything?"

I nodded, my eyes darting from the pasta pan to the pot with the chicken. "It all just needs stirring now. Until the sauce."

"Do you make the sauce?"

I turned my head back to look at him. Which was a mistake, because there was barely any space between us. One wrong move and my lips would be on his.

"No," I said slowly and softly. "You burned pasta. One thing at a time, Gordon Ramsey."

His lips twitched. Those gray eyes of his sparkled with silent laughter, and I turned around fully, gripping the overhanging edge of the countertop and standing on my tiptoes.

"You knew how to cut that onion, didn't you?" I asked quietly.

He nodded, his mouth now firmly in a smirking curve.

"And the mushrooms." I didn't bother asking this time.

"I said I can't cook, not that I can't cut." He lifted his hand to the side of my face and, after a brief hesitation, ran his fingers through my hair, leaving it to fan out as he reached the ends. "I thought you were supposed to be the strong one out of us."

"I'm the stupid one," I corrected him. "I genuinely thought you were that useless in the kitchen."

His laugh was quiet but deep, a genuine one that made goosebumps pop up on my arms. He rested his hands on the countertop next to me, his thumbs brushing across my little fingers, and he leaned forward just enough that I could feel his breath ghosting across my lips.

"Clumsy and easy to fool," he murmured. "How have you made it this far in adulthood?"

"I'm smart and scrappy," I breathed. "I could probably survive an apocalypse."

"After you'd fallen over a tree root or stubbed your toe on a rock." He lifted one hand to the side of my face. Slowly, he slid it around the side of my neck until his fingertips tickled the base of my scalp.

Shivers shot down my spine.

"At least I'd be able to eat." My voice was no more than a whisper, because his mouth was right there, barely an inch away, and my eyes were fluttering shut.

I could feel his lips.

There. Teasing mine. Seeing how far he could go before I'd stick to my guns and not kiss him.

He didn't have to go far.

"Shit!" I pushed him away and yanked the pot off the stove. "Goddamn it!"

The chicken was burned. We hadn't stirred it because he'd distracted me from what I was supposed to be doing.

Like not burn the goddamn chicken.

"Fuck it." I ran my hand through my hair. "It's screwed."

"Maybe we could…Oh, never mind." Jake wrinkled his nose and stepped back from it. "I thought you said you could cook."

"I don't usually have a hot guy distracting the hell out of me!" I dumped the pasta into the strainer in the sink and let the pan fall into the other side with a slam. "Well, this wasn't a mess at all."

Jake leaned against the table, grinning, with his thumbs hooked through his belt loops. "Shall I order a take-out?"

I sighed and looked at him. "You're gonna have to. I don't have any more pasta."

SEVENTEEN

UPSIDE#17: THE ONLY PERSON WHO GETS HOT IN YOUR KITCHEN IS YOU.

Lillie eyed me as I walked into the hotel. "Late night?"

"No. A sleepless one." I leaned against the counter, clutching my purse strap up onto my shoulder and keeping a tight hold of my coffee and donuts. "Anything I need to be aware of?"

"Quinn's sick and the bar order needs doing again."

I dropped my forehead onto the top of the desk. "No, no, no, no," I moaned. "I hate that order."

"I know, but you know if Harley does it, it'll just get all fucked up."

"I know," I moaned again. "But I hate it."

"What do you hate?" Jake wandered up to the counter and rested his arm on it.

Lillie turned to him with a big smile and pushed her hair away from her face. "The bar order."

He raised his eyebrows and turned to me. "Where's Quinn?"

Well, damn. He remembered her name.

"Sick," I replied, turning my head to the side.

"Who's supposed to do it in her absence?"

"Harley. But, she's not the best at it," Lillie added lightly.

She was also understating quite a lot…

He looked at her. "Isn't there anyone else who can do it? I have something I need Mellie to do today, so she doesn't have the time."

"You do?" I asked. "What?"

His eyes met mine. "I'll tell you in a minute. Where is Harley?"

I looked to Lillie.

She peered at her watch. "She should be behind the bar restocking. If not, she'll be in the storeroom."

Jake nodded once. "Are you coming?" he asked me.

"I, uh, sure." I shrugged, standing up straight. "I guess." I shot Lillie an uncertain look and followed Jake toward the bar.

"Why can't she do the order?" he asked quietly, leaning into me.

I shrugged again. "I don't know, honestly. She's not the newest, but she's the most full-time except for Quinn. For some reason, she just can't get it right."

"Why? What does she keep messing up?"

"The counts, mostly. I don't think she pays enough attention to what she's doing."

"Right." He stepped in front of me and, adjusting the collar of his shirt, walked around the side of the bar. "Harley?"

A scream came from the floor—then a smash.

Jake looked at me. "Don't say a word," he mouthed, pointing at me.

I hid a smile and looked down.

"Harley?" he tried again, this time a lot softer.

"Hi." She stood up, wiping her hands on her skirt and blushed. "Um, hi. Sorry. You scared me. Nobody usually comes in here this early."

Jake gave her a half-hearted smile. "You should probably sweep that glass up."

"Oh. Right. Of course." She laughed nervously and grabbed the dustpan and brush from under the bar. She bent down to sweep it up and dropped the glass into the small trash can. "I'll mop that up in a second. What's up?"

"The order needs to be done today, and I'm sure you're aware that Quinn called in sick," he started.

She swallowed and nodded. "Yeah. She texted me this morning." She fiddled with a loose thread on her shirt, looking down like she already knew where this was going.

"I'm going to need you to do the order this week. I have a couple things I need Mellie to do, so she won't have time to look it over." His tone was no-nonsense. "So, I'll need you to make sure it's accurate."

Her gaze went wild, like a kitten on catnip, almost. "Um, sure, okay. I can do that."

He raised his eyebrows. "Harley, I'm not going to lie, but you're not filling me with confidence that you can do this."

"I usually mess it up," she admitted.

Jake leaned forward, one hand on the bar. "Then, don't." He turned to me. "Mellie, shall we?"

I gave Harley a sympathetic smile and followed him back to the office. "That was a little...blunt," I said when he'd shut the door behind me. I put my coffee and donuts on the desk and sat down, setting my purse on the floor. "You could have been a little nicer."

Jake dropped into his chair. "No offense, Mellie, but you being nice is why she's unable to do the order. She knows that either you or Quinn will pick up the slack if she gets it wrong."

I couldn't argue with that. He was right. I'd been too soft on her as her boss. Instead of arguing, I sighed.

"This is the reason I started the employment review process. If doing the order in Quinn's absence is part of her job, then she has to be able to do it." He shrugged a shoulder and reached for a take-out cup of coffee on his side of the desk. "It's not your job to do it, just to place the order."

Once again, he was right.

"I know. What happens if she messes up?"

He met my eyes. "Then the roles have to be reviewed for the bartenders. If she can't do it, we'll get someone who can."

"You'd fire her?"

"No. I'd switch her job role with another member of staff who is capable of doing the order without needing their hand held. The renovation starts next week, and I need at least some of these guys to be able to do their jobs right."

It made sense. I didn't necessarily like it, but it was the right thing to do. "Okay. Fine. I don't like it, but fine."

"Don't tell them you don't like it."

I pulled my donuts out. "But that ruins the good cop, bad cop thing we have going on, doesn't it?"

"We don't have a cop thing going on."

"Oh, we do. You trying to cop a feel." I looked at him pointedly and bit into my donut.

He held his hands up. "Don't blame me if you couldn't see through my ruse. And I didn't try to cop a feel—if I wanted to, you'd have been putty in my hands."

"You're dreaming again," I said, biting into the donut again. "Not true."

Shaking his head, Jake sipped from his coffee. "You were almost putty. Admit it."

"Even if it were close to being remotely true," I said. "I would never admit it."

"Because it's true."

"It's not true!" I slammed my hand down right as the office phone rang. I snatched it up. "Mellie Rogers."

"Um, Mellie," came Harley's tentative voice. "There's a problem."

I sat bolt upright. "What is it?"

Jake frowned. "What?" he mouthed.

I hit the speaker button. "Harley. What's the problem?"

Jake covered his face with his hand.

"Um." She paused. "I was counting the tonic waters, and when I moved the top crate, it was wet, and…"

"Oh no."

"It slipped out of my hand and smashed."

It was my turn to put my hand over my face. "We'll be right there. How far into the order did you get?"

"That was the first thing I was going to count," she replied.

Jake sighed. "Leave the storeroom and go back to the bar. Call Rosa and ask if someone can run down to clean it. Mellie and I will do the order together this morning. But, be aware that we'll be having a meeting with Quinn when she returns."

I swear, I heard her gulp.

"Okay. I'll find Rosa now." She hung up. The line buzzed, filling the room with the awful sound, and I put the phone back on the unit before it annoyed me too much.

"Tell me one thing," Jake said, pinching the bridge of his nose. "How has this hotel been able to run with two complete klutzes working here?"

That was an excellent question.

<hr />

"Is that everything?"

I looked at the order form. It'd taken almost an hour to make sure the storeroom was completely clear of tonic water and glass from the bottles.

That was trickier than you'd think and didn't count the hours we'd spent actually doing the stock intake.

"I think so," I said, cringing at the extra-large number of tonic water we needed to order thanks to Harley's mishap.

"So, explain to me." Jake leaned against the side of the storage rack. "Why that's so hard for her?"

I shrugged and tapped the pen against the clipboard. "I don't know. It's not rocket science to count the bottles and see what we need more of."

"Like a hundred extra bottles of tonic," he muttered.

"Like a hundred extra bottles of tonic," I echoed. "Well, this is done. I can go and place it now."

"Finally." He pushed off the unit. "Here. Give me the keys. I want to check the floor for any remaining glass then I'll lock it behind us."

I dug the keys out of the pocket of my skirt and handed them to him. "Okay. I'll see you back in the office?"

"Sure."

I left him in the storage room and went back up to the office, making a quick detour to check on Harley. She'd been pretty shaken when I'd seen her on the way to the storeroom, mostly because Jake's way of telling her that her job would be changing was quite terrifying, and the poor girl probably thought she was about to be fired.

Thankfully, she seemed to have returned to normal when I'd seen her.

I sighed as I sat down at my desk. I was already tired of today, but mostly because I was realizing just how right Jake was.

The most annoying part was how the review thing was right. I'd been way too lenient with the bar order situation. Mostly because I hadn't ever followed up with Quinn that she'd been covering it with Harley, because she obviously hadn't.

"What are you thinking about?" Jake hovered in the doorway.

I looked up. "Did you find any glass?"

He shook his head. "The girls did a great job of cleaning the floor. Now, what's up?"

"I was just thinking," I said slowly. "About the review system."

"Here we go," he muttered, shutting the door.

"No, it's not bad." I ran my fingers through my hair. "It's—you're right," I said after a moment. "You're right."

He narrowed his eyes, coming over to me. "Did I just hear you tell me I'm right—twice?"

"You sure did." I slumped forward onto the desk. "You're right, Jake. I've been too relaxed when it comes to stuff being perfect around here. I should have made sure Harley knew how to do the order. I should have made sure Quinn had taught her it correctly and followed up after I knew she couldn't do it."

"That's why you have a face like a smacked ass?"

"You're not helping."

"Mellie, listen to me. It's not your job to make sure Harley knows how to do the order. It's Quinn's responsibility, and I'll be telling her that when she's back." He rounded the desk and leaned against it on my side. "Don't beat yourself up about it. You've been left to run this place pretty much single-handedly. I'm only making these changes because it's how I want this place to be run."

"I know that, but—"

"No, there are no buts." He gently nudged my shoulder so I sat up straight. "Look at me."

I gritted my teeth, but I did as he'd asked, turning my head to meet his eyes.

"You're not at fault here," he said quietly. "Trust me. I don't blame you. You can't oversee every single member of staff all the time. That's why you have other managers here. They're supposed to do it for you."

"I know, but—"

He pressed two fingers against my lips before quickly pulling them away. "I told you, no buts. You're a great manager, Mellie. I see the way you interact with all the staff and how much they respect you in turn. You're a wonderful person, and the only reason you haven't been hard on people is because you're just too damn nice."

"Being hard on people is part of my job," I said quietly, fiddling with a button on my shirt. "If I can't be honest with my staff and tell them more than once when I'm not happy, what kind of a manager does that make me?"

He pushed the hair from my eyes. "It makes you a great one. I know we've beaten the bar order to death and back to life, but here, listen to me." He put two fingers beneath my chin and tilted my head up so our eyes met. "You picked up the slack there because you didn't want anyone else to feel bad. You didn't have the time to do the order, but you did it anyway. You didn't want Harley to feel like she was failing, and you didn't want Quinn to think she wasn't training properly."

"But that's exactly what's happening."

"And it's my job to fix it." He stroked his thumb across my chin before pulling his hand back away. "I'm blunter than you. This is my hotel to fix, and when I'm done being bad cop, I know you'll be the good cop and put a smile back on everyone's faces."

"Smiles doesn't equal good work," I replied.

"No." His lips tugged up. "But what does equal good work is an amazing manager. One who has a smile for every staff member and goes out of her way to make sure the work environment is a happy one. You don't have to make sure everyone is doing their job perfectly. I want you to make sure everyone is happy."

I swallowed and looked down. "I want everyone to be happy. I want them to like coming to work here. I don't want them to go home feeling stressed or angry."

"Which is why you take care of the angry customers. You deal with the complicated phone calls. You handle all the paperwork and general running of the hotel, as well as making sure everyone has everything and there are no problems." His smile grew a little wider. "You buy them food and make sure the staff room gets a fresh flower delivery once a week. You buy their birthday presents out of your own money and make sure every member of staff gets a card at both birthday and Christmas. You cover shifts so others can leave early to see their wife have a baby or their sick aunt who's been rushed to the hospital."

I opened my mouth, but nothing came out. How did he know all that stuff? I didn't think anyone paid attention to the stuff I did. I knew it was appreciated, but I didn't know anybody actually cared enough to remember all the little things.

But, somewhere in this hotel, there were people who had.

"Rosa told me about the time her brother got in an accident while he was fishing, and you took the vacuum off her so she could go to the hospital, then she told me how you let her take the next day off because he was critical. And you sent her flowers, which she still feels bad about because she forgot to thank you."

"I didn't do it for thanks," I muttered.

"I know that, and so does she. Wake up, Mellie." He cupped my chin once again. "You don't need to make sure everyone does their job perfectly because you're too busy making sure this is a great place to work."

"How do you know all that stuff?"

He shrugged. "I asked when I first got here. My first impression of you was a bit of a hot mess—"

"That's changed?"

He paused. "Not particularly. You're still a hot mess, but you're an amazing hot mess."

"I'll take it."

A small laugh escaped him. "I asked the staff to tell me a little about you, and that's just a fraction of what I heard. You're not perfect. You break more stuff than the average person—"

"You sneak up on people. That's hardly my fault."

"You tell yourself that, spitfire." His eyes sparkled. "You break a lot of stuff, you're not always the brightest star in the sky when I mess with you—"

"Also not my fault."

He covered my mouth with his hand. "Stop fucking interrupting me."

I blinked at him. I couldn't agree to be quiet, could I?

I also couldn't breathe.

I peeled his finger away from my nostrils. "'An't breef,'" I said against his palm.

"Oh. Shit. Sorry." He dropped his hand with a laugh. "Can I finish now?"

I nodded.

"You break a lot of stuff, you're not always sharp when I'm being an idiot, and you're sometimes too nice and forgiving for your own good, but they're not bad things. They're just who you are, and I happen to think that who you are is pretty incredible." He ran his fingers through his hair. "Which is probably part of the reason why I can't stop thinking about kissing you every time I look at you."

A light flush rose up my cheeks. "This escalated quickly."

He took a deep breath in. "I stopped using my filter."

"It's been a long morning. I'll forgive you." My lips pulled into a half-smile, and I tucked my hair behind my ear. "Um...Thank you. I appreciate it?"

"Are you telling me? That sounded a lot like a question."

"I'm not used to anyone being so nice to me."

"Ironic, since you're the nicest person I've ever met."

"I literally spend half our conversations in a permanent state of sarcasm. That doesn't equal the nicest person you've ever met."

"How do you know? I've met some right assholes. Did I tell you about my cousin?"

I laughed, standing up. "You did. You've also met Peyton, and she's definitely a bigger asshole than I am."

"Most people are, spitfire."

Well, in his defense, he hadn't known me that long, really.

"Okay, so, what do we do about Harley?" I put my hands on my hips and leaned back against the windowsill. Before he could answer, I said, "I think we need to speak to

Quinn and explain there's obviously a training issue here, because, at the very least, she should have noticed that Harley struggles with it. She should have been taking Harley down to help when she's been doing the order. And if it's because Harley's not really number-inclined, then the task should have been taken off her a long time ago. I think Quinn needs to run through it all again with her and supervise her doing a couple of stock takes to find out the issue."

Jake raised his eyebrows, but he was smiling. "I see you were eager to hear my input."

"I don't like your attitude."

Laughing, he pushed off the desk and walked toward me. "Perfect." He tapped me on the nose. "That sounds like a good plan, spitfire."

"Can I ask you a question?"

"Other than the one you just asked?"

Cocky bastard. "Why do you call me spitfire?"

He tilted his head to the side, his eyes sparkling with something gentle but unidentifiable. "Because you are a spitfire. You're so gentle, but at the same time, you're incredibly fierce."

"Is that a good thing?"

He grinned, then briefly cupped my chin. "Yes. It is."

"Good to know." My eyes met his.

A storm brewed in his gray gaze. It was wild—a heady mix of want and restraint, of desire and determination.

I knew what he wanted to do.

My heart picked up a fast beat. I couldn't stop it, and after everything he'd said to me tonight, I knew he wanted to kiss me for more than one reason.

I wanted to kiss him.

I wanted to break the rule we'd set, the one I was so steadfastly determined to keep, and kiss him.

I didn't care that he was my boss. It was impossible to remember that when I looked into his eyes. All I saw was a guy, a regular guy, who wanted me. And it was tempting, intoxicating. None of the stuff we'd agreed mattered.

So, I broke the rule. That one rule I swore to myself I wouldn't break.

I kissed him.

I stepped forward, flattened my hands against his chest, and I kissed Jacob Creed.

His hands found my waist, his touch almost tentative, like he couldn't believe I was kissing him. As I slid my hands up his chest to his neck, he tightened his grip, making his fingers dig into my skin.

He pulled me against him so tight not even a breath could pass between our bodies. I wrapped my arms tight around his neck and kissed him hard. He responded in an instant, circling my body with one arm and bringing the other up to cup the back of my head.

His tongue flicked against my lips. I didn't hesitate in allowing him to deepen the kiss. I wanted more of him. I could feel him everywhere, from the taste of his coffee on his tongue to the effects of his kiss in the goosebumps on my arms.

I could feel him, too. His cock was hardening against my lower stomach, and he held me so tight there was no escaping it. Desire bolted through me as I gave in. There wasn't a part of my body that wasn't a raging inferno of need by the time he was fully hard.

If he pushed, I'd let him do more than kiss me.

I wanted him to push it. I wanted him to push it while I was so heady with lust that I couldn't think straight. I couldn't think anything at all except for him.

Couldn't think of anything but the way he gripped my hair. The way his fingers dug into my hip. The way my heart beat faster than I'd ever known it to before.

The way he kissed me.

He kissed me freely and with abandon, with pure passion that ricocheted right through my veins.

I was alive.

More alive than I'd ever been in the arms of a man.

And I was terrified of that.

Because it meant this was more than a schoolgirl crush. This was a real crush, one that tangled work politics with the heart, and that was a dangerous maze to navigate.

This was a real crush, based on an amazing guy with an even more amazing smile.

I broke the kiss, gasping. My thoughts had spiraled beyond just him, and now the reality of kissing him had shattered the momentary peace.

"I have to do the order before one," I breathed. It wasn't an excuse.

All right, it was, but it also wasn't a lie.

"Wait." He held me tight against him when I tried to move away. He ghosted his lips across my cheek to my ear and said, "You can't kiss a guy like that then run."

"Is there a rulebook for post-kissing etiquette?"

"I'll write one," he murmured, pulling back without releasing me. "Last night. Let's do it again."

I raised my eyebrows. "Where we try to cook, and you distract me so much the food burns?"

"Yes, but we skip the cooking and go straight to the distracting."

"The distracting is part of it—"

"Skip the cooking and go straight to fucking, Mellie."

Man. I really was dense.

I coughed. "That was, um, blunt."

He smirked. "I told you I'm blunter than you are."

"I'm determined to teach you how to cook. I'm not okay with skipping cooking."

"You're gonna burn it again."

"No. You're going to behave." I slid my hands down to his chest. "Since I assume this is non-negotiable."

He sighed. "I love it when you don't argue with me. I love it when you do argue with me, but since you have to do the order, it's easier that you aren't."

I pursed my lips.

He laughed and released his tight grip on me. "Look, I have to fly to my mom's tomorrow morning to help her pack up the last of my grandpa's things. I'll be back Friday. We can do it then."

"Do what? What are we categorizing this as? Clearly it's not non-friends."

"A date, Mellie. Call a date a date, would you?"

"That's a…I think you're supposed to ask to make it a date." My throat was dry. A date? Dear God. I wasn't prepared for a damn date.

"A non-date. That's a date." He crossed his arms, clearly fighting laughter.

"Just call it dinner and go away and let me do my job." I sat at my chair and booted the computer with a quick slap onto the keyboard. "Jake."

"You're so cute when you're awkward." He grinned again and straightened his shirt. "I'll leave you to it. I have a couple of things to do, then I have to go home and pack. Are you okay here?"

"I've handled it as the manager for the last four years. I think I'll be okay," I drawled.

Jake grabbed his jacket and winked. "I'll text you to set up Friday night, okay?"

I turned to the computer and hoped he wouldn't see me blush. "Okay."

"Oh, and, Mellie? You're really fucking cute when you blush like that."

I threw my wireless mouse at him.

Unfortunately for me, by the time the mouse got to him, he was already outside and had shut my door.

The mouse smashed into it and fell to the floor.

"Oh, shit!" I ran across the room and picked it up. The little light on the bottom flickered three times before going out. Not even turning it off and back on again worked.

I slumped against the wall and sighed. Hopefully, the nearest store wouldn't be too busy, and I could run in and out to get a new mouse.

My phone buzzed on the desk.

Jake: *I think you have an anger problem.*
Me: *I think I have a YOU problem!*
Jake: *I have a you problem. It's uncomfortable to sit in my car...*
Me: *Then stop being so hot and I won't accidentally kiss you.*
Jake: *Unfortunately, this level of good looking is hard to control. As for you "accidentally" kissing me, I'll take it. I did see you slip when you grabbed me...*

I huffed.

Me: *Go away. I have to go and buy a new mouse.*
Jake: *Anger problem...*
Me: *Go suck an alligator's ass.*
Jake: *Like I said...*
Me: *I'm going to watch Forensic Files tonight. Be afraid.*
Jake: *As long as I can fuck you first, you can kill me any way you like. I won't even put up a fight.*
Me: *GOODBYE, JACOB.*

I shoved the phone into my purse before the conversation could continue any further.

Yep. My problem was definitely Jake-sized.

EIGHTEEN

UPSIDE #18: THE ONLY FEELINGS YOU HAVE ARE TOWARD BABY ANIMALS. AND PIZZA.

"Do you ever stop working?" I asked, looking at Peyton tapping away on the phone.

"Seriously," said Chloe. "So much for girl's night."

Peyton sighed. "It's just one email."

"You said that five emails ago." I sipped my drink. "So, forgive me if I don't believe you, but I don't think you're putting that damn thing down anytime soon."

She peered at me over the table. A mischievous grin stretched across her face. "If you knew whose application I was looking at right now, you wouldn't be so frustrated."

Chloe leaned over to see her screen, but Peyton put her phone face down on the table.

I frowned at her, setting my glass back down. "I can honestly say that not once have I ever cared about your applications."

Her eyebrows shot up. "You would if you thought this ran in the family."

"If what ran in the family?"

In fact, I shouldn't have asked. Didn't Jake tell me that his cousin had a crush on Peyton?

Yes. Yes, he did.

"Well," Peyton started. "Let's just say he shares the same surname as your hot new boss."

Chloe gasped. "No!"

"Yes," Peyton said with a smug smile. "I just received an application from one Samuel Creed."

"Oh no," I groaned. "I didn't know he was serious."

Peyton picked up a glass and stared at me over the top. "You knew he was going to do this?"

"Um, maybe."

"I'm not mad, Mellie." There was a sparkle in her eye. "I've seen a lot of penises in the last couple of years, but I have to admit, that's a pretty darn nice-looking penis."

Chloe wrinkled up her nose. "There's no such thing as a nice-looking penis."

I had to agree. Nice was not a word I would use to ever describe a penis. "Sorry, Peyt. I'm with Chloe on this one."

Peyton shrugged her shoulders. "Look, all I'm saying is that if you think these things are genetic, they might just well be. If you were interested in a little more than your boss's ass."

"What the hell do you mean by that?" asked Chloe. "Actually, never mind. I don't think I want to know." She shook her head and reached for her glass.

Yeah. I was going to need more alcohol for this conversation.

Peyton laughed, holding her hands up. "Hey, hey. There may have been this one time in college that I accidentally slept with cousins."

Chloe spat out her drink.

"How…" I stared at her, then pinched the bridge of my nose for a second before composing myself. I looked up from my finished plate and met her eyes. "How do you accidentally sleep with cousins?"

"Yeah, I mean," Chloe started, then stopped. "How do you do that?"

"Well, obviously, I didn't know they were cousins." Peyton tucked her hair behind her ear. "I didn't meet them together. In fact, we couldn't have met any further apart."

"Wow, really?" Chloe said sarcastically. "That's the story you're going with?"

"Story? What do you mean, story? There's no story. I met one in class, and the other when I was on vacation for spring break."

"Okay," I said, looking straight at her. "Now, you have to be messing with us. That's the most ridiculous excuse I have ever had."

"It is not an excuse! God, it's not like I had a threesome with them." Peyton crossed her arms over her chest. "But, if you don't want to know about the genetic side of manhood, then that's fine by me."

Chloe glanced at me then back at Peyton. "Hey now, there's no need to be hasty about it. "Even if she doesn't want to know, I do."

"I didn't say didn't want to know." I pushed my plate to the side and brought my glass closer to me. "All I'm saying is that I don't really know how you can accidentally sleep with cousins."

"I clearly just explained that to you," said Peyton, sighing.

I rolled my eyes "Sure, but I didn't say that I believed you."

"Do you want to know or what?" Peyton asked sharply. "Because if you don't, I'm going to go back to work."

"God," Chloe said. "You suck at girl's night."

"Oh, just spit it out." I sipped the last of my cocktail. It was pretty obvious what she was going to say, and that was just from the sassy grin on her face.

"So." Peyton pushed her plate to the side and leaned forward, resting her forearms on the table. "Without going into too much detail—"

"Since when have you ever not gone into detail?" Chloe snorted.

"—It's worth noting," she paused, glancing around as if somebody could hear us. There are...similarities...in certain aspects of relative's bodies."

"Oh, boy. That was informative." I rolled my eyes again.

Peyton flipped me the bird across the table. I just laughed.

"Wait, wait, wait." Chloe leaned forward and stared at Peyton. "Are you telling me that male relatives have similar penis sizes?"

Peyton gripped the stem of her wine glass and glared at her. "And that was the detail I was hoping to avoid in a public place."

I frowned at her. She nodded toward the table next to us. With all the discretion of an atomic bomb, I looked sharply to my left.

Brilliant.

It was full of college-aged boys who were listening to every word we were saying.

Way to go, Chloe.

There was always one, and in this friendship, it was always Chloe.

With a heavy sigh, Peyton nudged my foot under the table, and we both turned to Chloe.

"Yes," Peyton said quietly. "Yes, that's exactly what I'm talking about, Chloe."

"Oh." Chloe blushed. "And, you're saying you just got a submission from her boss' cousin?"

Peyton grinned once again. "Sure did."

God. I'd never been more interested in anybody's penis in my life.

No, that was a lie. I was pretty sure I was damn interested in Tom Hardy's.

And, you know, she didn't exactly have to tell me anything about the penises of the Creed family, given that I'd had Jake's erection pressed against my stomach not forty-eight hours ago…

"Well," said Chloe. "You can't just leave it at that."

I hated to admit it, but she did have a point.

With a glance to the table of young guys next to us, Peyton leaned right into the middle of the table and motioned for us to do the same. "To put it simply, the only reason I'd kick him out of bed would be to fuck him on the floor."

"Well, luckily for you, he sent that in the hopes of getting your attention," I muttered. "He likes your boobs."

"They're pretty great boobs."

"I agree." One of the boys from the table next to us leaned over and gave her a devilish grin.

It was about as sexy as a mating pair of slugs.

"Oh, thanks." Peyton flattened her hand against her chest. "Now, stop looking, because the only place you'll ever touch them is in your dreams."

His friends all laughed at him, and she promptly turned her back on him.

I stared at her for a minute. "I'm trying to decide if a clapback like that to a guy a few years younger than you is cruel, or in this situation, totally justifiable."

"Totally justifiable," Chloe said. "We've seen Peyton eat bigger men for breakfast."

"Only when they taste good," she shot at her, then turned to me. "You seem real uninterested in Sam's dick. Do you know something about Jake that we don't know?"

I twirled my glass. "I'd hedge a guess that I know a lot of things about Jake that you guys don't."

Chloe smiled. "That's not what we're talking about, and you know it."

"Fine, but I'm not telling you anything until we've moved away from the pint-sized perverts." I shot a dark look at the guys at the table opposite us.

"Right, we're done, anyway." Peyton caught the attention of our server and motioned for the bill.

He brought it over minutes later, and we all threw down our share of the cash. Leaving it on the table, we gathered our things and headed out of the restaurant. We'd gone to our favorite place, and the walk down Bourbon Street reminded me of the first night I'd seen Jake.

The night they'd made me flash him. If I'd known then what I knew now, I sure as hell wouldn't have done it.

But you know what they always say about hindsight…

"All right. Now spit it out," Chloe demanded.

I took a deep breath. "We kissed."

"We know that." Peyton nudged me.

"No, again. We kissed again." I did a quick recap of how he'd basically tortured me into teaching him how to cook, then how he'd decided he didn't want to cook, and seducing me was the best option.

"I'm a little turned on," Chloe muttered.

"Oh, I'm not done." I carried on and went through what had happened at work two days ago and what was happening tomorrow night. "I'm not even going to see him until what he insists is a date."

Peyton tapped her finger against her lips. "Are you sure dating your boss is a good idea? I mean, I'm all for using men for my own pleasure—"

"And you wonder why you're single," Chloe interjected.

"Hey, they use me, too. It's all mutual." Peyton pointed out before returning her attention back to me. "Have you thought this through? The implications of working with your boss? I mean, not even a co-worker. Your boss."

"Only a thousand times."

"Other than she's a chicken, there's a reason Chloe hasn't told Dom how she feels."

Chloe ground her teeth together. "There's nothing to tell."

"Sweetie, your denial does nothing to convince us," I told her. "We know you're in love with him, so give it a rest."

She glared at both of us before turning away.

Peyton rolled her eyes. "I just—I've seen it go wrong. Do you know how many women come to me and tell me they hooked up with someone they worked with?"

"She does have a point," Chloe agreed begrudgingly. "We get those stories all the time. Seriously. The Stupid Cupid application box is full of them. The number of interviews we do where we have both men and women say to us, 'Oh, I had a bad break-up with a co-worker, now I have a new job, and I'm looking for a new relationship, blah, blah, blah.' It's wild, Mellie."

"Geez, you guys, I'm not saying I want the guy's babies. You're the ones who made me tell you this. Do you have anything supportive to offer me at all?" I peered at them both.

"Yes. Don't do it," Peyton said.

"You changed your tune," Chloe said to her. "Weren't you all for it before?"

"Yes. That was before I looked at Starstruck Sally over here and realized she isn't going to screw him and move on. Haven't you noticed the stupid grin on her face when she talks about him?"

"I do not get a stupid grin! And Starstruck Sally? What the hell?" I prodded her arm.

"Yeah," Chloe said. "I noticed the grin."

"It's the same one you get when we mention my brother," Peyton responded.

"One day, when you sleep, I will kill you."

"Guys, we've had this narrative now for ten years. Can we focus on my problem? I'm sure we've got another couple of years to nail Chloe about her undying love for Dom."

"I don't know why I'm friends with you people," Chloe snapped.

Peyton linked her arm through Chloe's. "Because I make mean cocktails, and Mellie can cook anything with a blindfold on."

Perhaps a slight exaggeration, but yes. That was the general reasoning.

I walked around and linked my arm through Chloe's other one. Her cross-body purse bumped into my leg, but I didn't mind. "Help me out. I don't need advice from Panty-Dropper Pamela over there."

Peyton laughed.

"You're the dating expert. Tell me what to do."

Chloe took a deep breath and thought about it for a moment. "Well," she said slowly. "It's tough because you work together. If we matched clients and found out they worked in the same company, we'd be hesitant to go through with it. They almost always end badly and awkwardly, mostly because the biggest thing those two people would have in common is work. Which means most of their conversation would be about work."

"That makes sense."

"But, it's a little different with you and Jake. I mean, there's clearly a real chemistry there, and you're both clearly too attracted to each other to ignore it." She clicked her tongue. "So…I don't know what to say. If I tell you to run away, I don't think you'll be able to, because even if you deny it, I think you're starting to get real feelings for him."

I wanted to deny it. I really did. I wanted to laugh at her and tell her to stop being so stupid, but I couldn't.

She was right.

I did have feelings for him. They were small, but they were big enough to be undeniable. Strong enough that one more kiss, one more laugh, one more touch, and they could flourish into something more.

And that scared me. A lot.

I didn't want to fall for my boss. I didn't want to feel the way I felt when I was around him. And that was just now.

What would happen in a week, a month, a year from now? If these feelings didn't go away, I was screwed, completely and utterly screwed.

Not in the good way. The bad way.

Jake was determined to pursue something. I had a constant battle inside me. My head told me no, to run, but my heart told me to ignore my stupid head and listen to it instead.

My heart obviously forgot that time in senior year where it got itself broken.

Fickle little bitch.

"Your silence is telling," Peyton said softly.

"I just...I don't want to be in a situation where my job is at risk." Although did I truly believe that? After everything he'd said to me, did I believe that would ever be the case?

Not right now, but that didn't mean that couldn't change. That didn't mean that wouldn't change. And if it did, there would be nothing I could do about it.

The hotel was his new baby, and I was just a staff member.

What if we started a relationship and then it all fucked up? He wouldn't leave. He couldn't quit. I'd have to be the one to do it.

And I didn't want to do that.

"Then, you have to decide," Chloe said, squeezing my arm. "Is the way you feel worth the risk? Is Jake worth the risk?"

Talk about a loaded question.

"I don't know," I admitted softly. "I really don't know."

NINETEEN

UPSIDE #19: YOU GET TO KEEP ALL THE CHANGE YOU FIND DOWN THE BACK OF THE SOFA. UNLESS IT'S TAX SEASON, THEN YOU CAN KISS THAT THREE DOLLARS AND SIXTY-TWO CENTS GOODBYE.

"How was your trip?" I cradled the glass of wine and leaned against the small island in the kitchen of Jake's apartment.

"As well as it could have gone," he admitted, setting the wine bottle down on the granite countertop. "My mom is still struggling with some grief, but I think it might ease for her now the house is cleared and on the market."

"I'm glad it went well." I smiled.

"How is everything at the hotel? I didn't get a chance to stop by thanks to my flight delay."

"It's fine. Quinn seems to have Harley shadowing her a lot more, so hopefully, that works out." I shrugged a shoulder.

Jake sipped from the glass and walked around the island to me. "Good to know."

"You don't really want to talk about work, do you?" I met his gaze and kept it as he came right up to me. I turned as he approached, and in what was fast becoming a signature move, he trapped me against the island, his thumbs brushing my hips.

"Not really," he said in a low voice. "I can talk about work with you at work."

"Oh. That makes sense." I swallowed. It also went against the fear that work would overshadow any potential relationship.

Damn it.

"What are we cooking tonight?" His eyes glittered, and his lips pulled up into a one-sided smirk. "Gumbo? Jambalaya?"

"Woah, Gordon Ramsay. Slow down." I put my hands flat against his chest and pushed back at him. "Maybe we should try not to burn pasta before we try something a little more complicated."

"It's like you don't trust me to cook."

"You. Burned. Pasta." I punctuated each word with a jab of my fingertip into his chest.

"Hey, hey!" He grabbed hold of my finger. "Watch where you're poking that thing."

"You burned pasta, and you want me to teach you how to make classic New Orleans food? No. Boil pasta first." I pushed his arm away and walked over to where the grocery bag from my shopping trip was. "Boil the water, and if you can do this successfully, we'll see about something more complicated next time."

"Hell, it's like being seven again."

"Did you burn pasta at seven?"

"I wasn't allowed to make toast at seven."

I put the pasta on the side and stared at him. "You weren't allowed to put toast in a toaster at seven?"

"Nope. Almost set the toaster on fire once." He tucked his hands in the pockets of his light jeans and grinned.

"How—never mind. I don't want to know how you did that." I shook my head and turned back to the unpacking. I pulled out the chicken, onion, peppers, mushrooms, and garlic, followed by a jar of sauce.

That's right. It was cooking lesson one, take two.

I hoped we'd get it quicker than movie outtakes seemed to.

"Fill a pan with water and boil it," I told him.

"A pinch of salt," he said, pulling out a pan from a cupboard. "Not a tsunami of it."

Ah, we were getting somewhere.

He managed to get through salting the water and putting it to boil with overfilling the pan being his greatest mishap.

And he called me clumsy. Seriously.

At least I could boil water.

"I'll cut the onion and pepper," I told him. "We're not repeating last time."

"But last time was fun."

I pointed a knife at him. "Behave yourself."

He leaned against the side. "This is the worst non-date that's a date if I have to behave myself."

"You're the one who started this. You wanted me to come here. I'd rather be at home with a take-out."

He clutched his hand to his chest. "You break my heart, spitfire."

"You talk shit, bossman."

He grinned. "That's kind of kinky."

"Only if you assume I'm less feisty between the sheets." I froze, staring at the tiled backsplash. Why the hell did I say that?

"I assumed you were feisty all around." His grin turned wolfish, playful, but also deadly sexy.

I pulled the chicken out of the packet, dropped it on the cutting board, and sliced the knife right down the middle of it without looking.

He winced.

Now, it was my turn to grin.

I carried on with dicing the chicken while he watched the water boil. It was weird—there was an awkwardness in the air that had never been present before. It hung heavily, dripping off most of our words, and I was almost afraid to move toward him in case it was too much.

Two days. It'd been two days since he'd walked out of the office after I'd kissed him. Two days since I'd had revelations about how I looked at him, about how I felt about him.

Apparently, two days was long enough to create a divide between two people who were stuck between a rock and a hard place.

I didn't really know what to say to him. I didn't know how to act around him.

What was this?

Why wasn't I able to categorize it?

Was I not strong enough to make the choice?

Did I need him to help? Did that make me weak? Or was this something we needed to name together?

There was only so long the non-date-date could stick around. Sooner or later, we'd cross the line of messing around and something would become serious.

What if we already had?

What if this was beyond a laugh? Beyond a game, beyond something we could come back from?

I took a deep breath and dumped all the chicken into the big pot he'd placed on the stove top. He moved out of the way so I could clean the board and the knife and my hands, and I didn't make eye contact on my way to the sink or on my way back to the side where the mushrooms were waiting for me.

This was decidedly less sexy than before.

There was none of him touching me. None of the cutting with his hand over mine. None of his breath fluttering my hair.

He was on the other side of the kitchen.

I wished he wasn't.

I wanted him to be over here with me. "Could you put some oil in this pan and start the chicken?"

"Sure." He paused. "I don't know where the oil is."

I paused and pinched my nose. "You don't have oil, do you?"

"Uhh…"

I stepped back and glanced at the sides. Nope. No oil. Not even in the cupboard above me. "Butter?"

"I have butter." He opened the fridge and handed me some. "You're going to cook chicken in butter?"

Using the knife, I sliced some butter out of the tub and dropped it right into my pan. "You need to add the pasta. And *stir it*, Jacob."

"Yes, Melanie."

"Don't call me Melanie."

"Don't call me Jacob."

"Stop arguing with me!"

"Only if you stop arguing with me."

There went the awkwardness.

"You're such a child." I chopped the top off the pepper and pushed it to the side ready to cut it in two and dice it. "I know you're doing this just to annoy me."

"No, if I wanted to annoy you, I'd be helping you chop that pepper." He laughed, stirring the pasta.

I slid my gaze toward him. "Look at you, behaving yourself," I drawled. "You're full of shit, Jacob Creed."

"You want me to help you do the pepper?"

I sliced out the middle then cut it into two. "I'm good, thank you."

"I thought you were teaching me how to cook."

"I'm teaching you how to boil pasta. After the last attempt, be thankful I'm doing that damn much."

He laughed, stirring it again. "I get it. I get it. Cook the pasta and we can discuss more."

"Exactly."

"What exactly are we discussing when the pasta is done?"

"Next week's roster," I shot back, cutting the pepper into chunks before throwing it into the pan. I stirred it. "How does that sound?"

"Like the worst date ever."

"This isn't a date."

"Says you."

"Yes, says me. It's not a date."

He put the wooden spoon on top of the pan and walked over to me.

"Nuh-uh." I swapped my knife for the spoon. "I'm not burning this again because you can't follow the rules."

"Weren't you the one who kissed me last time?"

"I didn't know we were keeping score. If so, you're losing." I shoved him to the side so I could cook the chicken properly.

"How am I losing?"

"Because of all the times we've kissed, you've kissed me more than I have you."

"I think you'll find we're even, spitfire."

"We sure aren't."

He threw the wooden spoon onto the side and stared at me so intently I had no choice but to meet his gaze. "The first time we kissed was an accident. The first time was all me. The second time was all you. That makes us even."

I sniffed. "You moved in for the kiss the first time."

"I went to kiss your cheek. How did I know you'd run away at the same time?"

"I was under the impression the night was over. That wasn't running away. That was going home—especially since your cab had shown up."

"Accident. It was an accident. That means we're even."

I didn't like being even.

Instead of responding, I huffed, ignoring his response in favor of making sure the chicken cooked right through. If I were a fuse, he was a match, waiting to set me on fire. And I wasn't going to give in to the burn that was his argument.

I had better things to do.

Like not burn the fucking chicken.

I gave all my attention to that pan, occasionally looking up to the pasta one where Jake was actually remembering to stir it. I didn't know whether or not it was because we weren't distracting each other or because I was still feeling so damn awkward, but I didn't care.

Stir. Stir. Stir.

Focus on the chicken. On unscrewing the jar. On pouring in the sauce. Focus, focus, focus. Focus on the goddamn chicken.

Not on the hot guy next to me, stirring pasta like he's stirring a gossip pot. Anything to keep it from sticking.

That was all I could pay attention to. I stirred on autopilot, but my eyes were trained on him. On his arm. On the way his muscles flexed, on the way the veins in his forearm moved with each twist of his wrist.

I couldn't stop staring. I was obsessed. It was mesmerizing; the way shadows moved across his skin as his wrists bent and his fingers clenched the spoon.

I was in trouble if I was getting turned on by a man stirring pasta.

Big, big trouble.

"Stare a little more, spitfire. You might burn a hole in my arm." Jake glanced over at me with a smirk. "You're as obvious as a case of crabs."

I stopped, mid-stir. "How do you know how obvious crabs is?"

"I watch television. Also, Sam's a whore," he answered without batting an eyelid.

"Is that a direct quote I can take to my friend who thinks his cock is pretty?"

Jake wrinkled his face up. "As the proud owner of a cock, I'm certain they're not pretty."

"Maybe yours drew the ugly straw. How many cocks have you seen?"

"Communal showers in high school and college after football games. Do you need more information?"

"That was already too much, thanks." I turned off the stove. "We're done here. Can you drain that?"

Jake looked in the pan. "You mean I cooked pasta without burning it?"

"We'll see when you drain it." I pushed my pan off the heated burner and watched as he poured pasta out of the pan and into the drainer. None was stuck to the bottom. That was quite the feat, considering I was sure I still had some of his stuck to mine…

"Make sure all the water is out of it," I told him. "Then you can tip it into my pan."

He looked momentarily confused, but he shook the shit out of that pasta until no water was coming out. Seconds later, he put the pasta into my pan, and I slid it back onto the burner to heat it all through.

"Cheese?" I asked.

He dumped the drainer in the sink. "There's an awful lot of you doing the cooking here tonight."

I glanced over my shoulder. "At least you didn't burn the pasta this time."

He snatched the block of cheese from the fridge and slammed the door shut. "You know something? My mother would love you, you little smartass."

"People do tend to fall in love with me," I said snarkily. "It's either my ability to blush at eye contact or break something within ten feet of me."

"No kidding," he muttered. "I'm amazed you've been in this kitchen long enough without breaking something."

"I'd be happy to make your leg the first thing."

"Do you want me to grate this cheese or slice it?"

That's what I thought, too.

Jake moaned as he leaned back into the sofa. "You're a pretty good cook, you know that?"

"Aw, don't give me all the credit. You rocked that pasta."

"You literally just showed me a Facebook video about a kid who made a full-blown carbonara from scratch, including the pasta and the sauce." He rolled his head to the side and stared at me.

"Okay, but in his defense, he was Italian."

"That's a defense?"

"It's basically a crime to use a jar of sauce in Italy."

"Why did you just use one?"

I blinked at him. "I'm not Italian, and you were an idiot about pasta until an hour ago."

He opened his mouth, paused, and reconsidered his argument. "Point well made."

"At least you didn't burn the pasta this time."

He raised his wine glass in salute of that acknowledgment. "To progress!"

I giggle-snorted my wine, and it went up my nose, burning somewhere between my brain and my eyes. I reached to put the glass on the table.

My eyes were shut, and I had no idea how far away the table was from my hand. No, instead of looking like a regular human being, I flapped one hand in front of my face.

And spectacularly failed at putting the glass on the table with the other hand.

There was a dull thud as the glass hit the ground.

I froze, the bones in my skull still feeling like they were burning. Dear God, when would it stop? Why wouldn't it stop? One wine-snort didn't deserve this much torture.

"I broke it, didn't I?" I said thickly, pinching my nose.

"Surprisingly," Jake said brightly. "No. But, I'm really glad that's white wine and not red wine."

"Oh no. It went on the rug, didn't it?"

"On the rug, up your nose…It's all relative with you at this point, spitfire."

This man had a horrible habit of being right. I was really beginning to get tired of it.

That, or he knew me far too well for my liking.

In fact, to make it fair, I was getting damn tired of both.

"Oh God," I muttered, finally letting go of my nose. The burn was subsiding to an uncomfortable sting, and I was able to concentrate on what was going on.

I don't know what he was saying about being glad the wine was white. There hadn't been that damn much left anyway.

Anyone who spilled a wine glass with more than a mouthful in had to be sentenced to treason, surely.

Jake set a towel on the rug to wipe up the worst of the wine, then scrubbed it with a wet cloth. I sat on the sofa, legs crossed, grimacing as I watched his arm muscles flex back and forth.

Grimacing because it was oddly hot.

I rolled my shoulders and picked up the empty glass from the rug. It really was just a splash and thank God for that. Any more and I'd have to hate myself.

"Now," he said. "Do I get you another, or has Queen Clumsy had enough?"

"Look." I pointed my empty glass at him. "There's something to be said for the pain of snorting wine up your nose."

"Better wine than cocaine."

I stopped, mouth open ready to respond. His response was so quick and sharp and, holy shit, I'd only gone and met my fucking match.

"I don't know how to reply to that at all," I said.

"I was looking on the bright side." Jake picked the bottle of wine from the door of the fridge and brought it over. He poured enough wine into my glass to fill it halfway then set the bottle on the table. "If I give you this, do you promise not to drop it?"

"No."

He laughed and passed me it. "Of course, you can't."

I took a sip and put it on the table—actually getting it on there this time.

"So, when will you teach me to cook properly?"

I stared at him. "How many times do I have to tell you that you just boiled pasta? When you can do that without supervision, we can try something harder."

"Then it's a weekly thing."

"Wait, what?"

Jake grinned. "You teaching me how to cook."

"You know there's a cooking channel, right? Or, like, YouTube. Or Google. There are lots of places you can learn to cook." I paused. "You only want me to teach you how to cook so you can touch my ass."

"Well, technically, I can touch your ass whenever."

"No, you can't." I met his eyes. "I mean, you can, but you can't."

"You make no sense."

"You're the one who claims you can touch my ass whenever you want."

Another grin stretched across his face. "That's because I can. I'll prove it if you want me to."

"I don't want you to prove anything."

"Then, stop fighting with me about it."

"If I stop, that means you're right."

"I am right."

I glared at him. "You're not right."

"You don't even know what we're talking about anymore, do you?" His eyes sparkled.

"No, but I know you're wrong about whatever it is."

Jake slid across the sofa so he was right next to me.

"What are you doing?" I pushed myself against the arm of the sofa.

"Proving you wrong, and me right." He grabbed hold of me, pulling me closer to him. My heart beat a little faster as he wrapped one arm right around me. His hand slid down my back to my hip, rounding over my ass. "See? I'm right."

Ah, shit. We were talking about him being able to touch my ass.

And here he was, touching my ass.

I swallowed. His fingers dug into my ass cheek, and he pulled me tighter against him. My hand rested against his solid stomach, and I could feel the dips of lightly toned abs beneath my fingers.

I flicked my tongue out over my lower lip as my gaze raised to meet his. Desire stared back at me, and I shuddered out a breath as he pulled me over on top of him.

"What are you doing?" I whispered.

"Kissing you." He cupped the back of my neck, and before I could respond, pulled my face down to his.

Our lips met. My heart instantly thudded against my ribs, and I slipped my hands up to cup his neck. My knees were nestled on the sofa on either side of his body, and he held me tight against him.

His cock hardened in seconds. It pushed against my clit, sending a burst of desire through me. Inadvertently, I thrust my hips, pressing myself against him.

Jake deepened the kiss. He fisted my hair, tugging lightly, his tongue flicking against mine, almost as if he was asking for more. A tiny whimper escaped my lips, and I grabbed the neck of his shirt.

I wanted to pull it off. I wanted to tug it up over his head and run my hands across his skin, touching each one of the muscles on his stomach. I wanted to sweep my hands across his broad shoulders and down his toned arms.

And I wanted more.

I didn't just want his shirt off.
I wanted it all off.
And damn it, I was going to take it all off.

Jacob

UPSIDE #20: THE ONLY PERSON WHO GETS TO HOLD YOU ACCOUNTABLE FOR YOUR ACTIONS IS YOURSELF. UNLESS YOUR COUSIN WALKS IN ON YOU KISSING THE PERSON YOU SHOULDN'T BE.

I gripped Mellie's ass, pulling her right against me. For someone who was so determined not to kiss me, she was grabbing onto me like her life depended on it. She was tugging on my shirt so hard I was certain she was going to try to take it off me.

And I didn't fucking care.

My cock pressed against her pussy, and every now and then, she twitched her hips, moving them against me like she wanted more.

I wanted more.

Would she let me? Would she let me pull that shirt over her head and kiss down her collarbone? Would she let me flip her over on her back on this sofa and kiss a trail down her body to where I wanted her most?

She gave a little moan into my mouth, one that vibrated across my skin and made my cock twitch.

I loosened my grip on her ass and trailed my fingers up her back, taking the material of her shirt with me. Her skin was hot under my touch, and she shivered.

I pulled back slightly, smiling against her lips. She drew in a deep breath, quickly letting it back out before she kissed me again.

Fuck, I loved kissing her. Her lips were soft and full, and she responded to every little thing I did. Whether it was my tongue against hers or my fingers dancing across her skin, she reacted.

I wanted to know how else she'd respond to me.

If her toes would curl if I put my tongue on her clit. If she'd arch her back or dig her nails into me as she came.

If she'd scream or shout.

If she'd beg and ask for more.

I needed to know.

I pulled her shirt up higher, and the lock on the door clicked.

"Oh shit!" Mellie jumped off me onto the sofa cushion next to me.

I quickly adjusted my pants, resisting the urge to shove a cushion on my lap. That was a fucking rookie movie, and really, it wasn't me that was the problem. It was Mellie.

Her hair was a mess where I'd had my hand in it. Her lips were swollen and pink, not to mention her cheeks were flushed almost red.

And her eyes.

They shone. Bright and wild. They flitted back and forth between me and the door as it swung open, revealing Sam with a short redhead hanging off his arm.

She giggled, and he froze as his eyes landed on me. I glared at him.

"Ah, fuck," Sam said under his breath. "I forgot."

Mellie cleared her throat and smoothed her hair down with her fingers. "It's—it's fine. I have to go anyway. I start early tomorrow."

I raised an eyebrow and looked at her. "You don't start until ten-thirty."

"Um, no. I changed it. I have to do that—that thing." She grabbed her purse from the armchair and slipped her feet into her shoes.

"What thing?" I sat forward, shuffling to the edge of the sofa.

"The thing!" she snapped, running her hands through her hair again. "I'll see you tomorrow."

Sam pulled tonight's plaything to the side. Mellie passed him without looking up, and the second she was out of sight, I glared at him.

The redhead looked between us uncertainly. "Uh, do you mind if I use your bathroom?"

"Sure, babe. Down the hall and it's the second door on the right." He smacked her ass.

She giggled, offering me an awkward smile, and teetered through the room on sky-high heels.

"How much is she costing you?" I snapped, standing up and grabbing the wine bottle. I walked it into the kitchen and grabbed the cork from the island to close it.

"Shut up." He slammed the door shut. "I'm sorry, all right? I forgot she was here."

"No, you thought with your dick instead of your head."

He threw his arms out. "She's your fucking employee, Jake. You said yourself it was a bad idea. Really, I was doing you a favor."

I put the bottle back in the fridge and shoved it closed. "No, you fucking weren't. Employee or not, I like her a lot. Jesus, Sam, I put up with this shit almost every night." I motioned toward the bathroom. "You couldn't give me one evening alone here?"

"She's. Your. Employee." He slammed his hand against the island with each word. "Remember that? Someone you hire? Someone you pay? Someone you tell what to do?"

I stared at him for a moment, then shook my head. I knew that. I knew she was my goddamn employee, but I didn't care.

I wanted her more than I'd ever cared about it.

"I'm going out." I walked to the front door, put on my sneakers, then grabbed my jacket off the hook.

Sam looked at me, holding his hands out.

"I'm not listening to another one of your fuck marathons," I told him. "You can stand there and judge me for falling for my employee, but you're twenty-eight and fucking random women like you're being paid to do it. Worry about your relationships before you worry about mine."

I yanked open the door and slammed it behind me. I shrugged on my jacket and headed for the stairs.

It was like living with an eighteen-year-old.

I had to find my own fucking apartment.

⊸•⊶

I opened the new carton of orange juice and stared at it.

I wasn't usually a straight-from-the-carton guy. It would be petty as fuck, but I was in a petty mood despite the fact I was a grown-ass man.

I pushed my unused glass to the side and drank straight from the carton. Fuck Sam and his interruption. He'd not only interrupted my date, but he'd left me with such a case of blue balls he'd interrupted my sleep.

That was the only reason I'd jacked off in the shower at three a.m. Fuck knew I wasn't getting any sleep until I'd got the frustration out of my system.

If he hadn't come in, Mellie and I would have finished what we started. I would have been able to carry her into my room and fuck her until this morning.

I recapped the carton and put it back in the fridge. I got a pathetic fizzle of amusement from closing the fridge with the carton in there.

"Oh. I'm sorry. I didn't know anyone was awake."

I turned and looked at the redhead Sam brought home last night. She was wearing nothing but an old t-shirt of Sam's that I recognized from high school, and her hair was pulled up on top of her head. Makeup was smudged beneath her eyes, and she looked a million miles away from the person she did last night.

"Early start at work," I said. "Where's Sam?"

"Still asleep." She cocked a thumb over her shoulder awkwardly and shuffled.

Trust it to Sam to piss me off then leave me to babysit his mess.

"Can I get you anything? Coffee? I think there's herbal tea somewhere," I offered.

"Uh, do you have juice?"

I motioned toward the fridge. "There's a bunch in there. Help yourself."

"Thanks. Where are your glasses?"

Yep. Definitely babysitting.

"I just took that from the dishwasher. I have to go, so knock yourself out." I smiled at her and grabbed my phone.

"Oh, okay, thanks. Bye." She opened the fridge, and when I looked back before I left, I saw her pull the orange juice carton out.

I fought back a smile and left the apartment. Petty as fuck, but who wasn't sometimes? I still had serious blue balls because of my cousin, and she was part of that by default.

I rubbed my hand across my forehead and stepped out onto the sidewalk. It was so quiet for such a big city, but then again, it was eight in the morning. The only people awake were the people like me who had to work instead of party until all hours.

I made the ten-minute walk to the hotel and used the passage at the side to go in through the back entrance. No matter what I'd said to Mellie, there were still a few staff members wary of me and the review system I'd put in place.

I didn't care; I just didn't feel like getting evil eyes this early in the damn morning.

It was almost as if some of the staff thought that killing me with their gazes would make their jobs way more secure.

Apparently, I had more than a couple of idiots working for me.

I sighed and stopped outside the office. I'd been so determined to get here that I hadn't stopped for coffee.

Or donuts.

I had a feeling a certain somebody would need donuts after last night.

Giving up on the staying away from staff thing, I walked out to the lobby where Lillie was helping someone check out at reception. I hovered at the end of the desk and waited for her to be done, all the while admiring how good she was at her job.

She was a lot like Mellie—she just made people feel good. Even if Lillie did stumble over her words with me sometimes.

"Hey," I said when she was done. "How are you doing?"

"Morning!" she said brightly. "I'm good. How are you?"

"Good, thanks. Is Mellie here yet?"

Lillie nodded. "She got here about ten minutes ago. She's in a—hey, I didn't see you come in."

"I came in the back. You said Mellie's here?"

"Yeah, she's in y'all's office. She's in a real bad mood, though, so I'd avoid going in there."

I raised my eyebrows. "She is?"

"Yep. She didn't speak to anyone on her way when she got here, and I'm pretty sure we all heard the door slam." She paused and looked at me, her eyes narrowing slightly. "She said she was seeing you last night. What did you do to her?"

Great. She's in a bad mood, and everyone assumes it's my fault.

Lillie wasn't everyone, but fuck me.

"I didn't do anything." I held up my hands. "We just did dinner, no big deal."

"Hmm. You two spend a lot of time together."

This was getting awkward really quickly.

"Uh…" How the hell did I respond to that?

"Is something going on with you two?"

"I'm not sure that's any of your business…" I trailed off. "Did she have breakfast with her when she came in?"

Lillie leaned on the counter and folded her arms on it before grinning at me. "Something is going on with you two."

"Did she have breakfast with her?" I asked again, stepping to the side.

"No, she didn't. No coffee, either, if you were wondering."

"Perfect, thanks." I tapped the top of the desk and headed for the front door.

"I like coffee, too!"

"Got it!" I called, holding my hand up in acknowledgment.

I went to Mellie's favorite coffee shop a block away. After grabbing three coffees and enough powdered donuts to put her in a sugar coma, I headed back to the hotel. I slipped Lillie's coffee behind the desk, and she shot me a thumbs up in thanks.

Then I braced myself for what was sure to be a hurricane behind the office door.

I went for the handle, but it was locked. Surely if she'd left, Lillie would have said something? Then again, she was busy talking to someone…

I put the donuts down and dug my key out of my pocket. I couldn't get it fully inside the keyhole, which meant Mellie had her key in it.

She'd locked me out.

I pulled my key out, stuffed it back inside my pocket, and knocked on the door. "Mellie?"

She didn't answer.

"Mellie, I know you're in there."

Still nothing.

"Let me in."

There was the sound of something moving inside, but she didn't respond to me.

I knocked. "Mellie, open the damn door and let me inside."

Nothing. She was completely and utterly ignoring me, and I was already running out of patience. However, I did have one last trick in my arsenal.

"I have donuts."

Silence.

Then, slowly, the sound of someone moving toward the door and the lock clicking.

Thank God for that.

Donuts really were the key to her.

I opened the door and picked up the donuts to carry inside. She was already sitting back at her desk with her feet up. She had a paper file open on her lap, and there were a few marks and circles written on it.

I kicked the door shut behind me. "Hey."

She glanced over at me. "Hey."

"I got you coffee. And donuts." I put the bag on the desk and set the coffee down in front of her. "I already had breakfast, so they're all yours."

"Thanks." She didn't look at me. She was fully focused on whatever paperwork she had in front of her, and I wasn't sure anything I could say would bring her attention to me.

She was angry. There was no doubt about it. It rolled off her in waves, like the after-effect of a tsunami, except my gut told me the tsunami hadn't yet hit.

I wouldn't push her right now. I'd give her a little time to calm down, but we had to talk about what had happened last night. We had to talk about what would have happened.

Even if I never got to kiss her again, we had to clear the air.

We had to make this a place we could work together.

Feelings or no feelings.

TWENTY-ONE

Mellie

UPSIDE #21: YOU DON'T HAVE TO EXPLAIN YOUR ANGER TO ANYONE BUT THE PILLOW YOU PUNCH TO DEATH.

I could feel his eyes on me.

They burned.

No matter how hard he tried to not look at me, it seemed as though he was incapable of it, just like I was when it came to ignoring the fact he was looking at me.

I didn't want to talk to him. I hadn't even wanted to let him in here, as evidenced by me putting my key in the door to stop him.

Damn him for bringing me donuts, though. As soon as he said that, I was weak.

I reached over for the bag and pulled out one of the donuts. The powder went everywhere, but I bit into it anyway without caring.

I didn't know why I was so angry. It wasn't that his cousin had walked in. I didn't care about that.

Okay, I was a little annoyed about that. Just a little.

I lied. I did know why I was angry.

I was angry at myself. I was angry because I'd let it get that far. Not only had I let us go so far, I was willing to go further. I wanted to go further. He was my damn boss, and I'd been sitting on top of him, willing to let him fuck me if he really wanted.

And he had. I'd felt that. I knew he wanted it.

Maybe that was why I couldn't look at him. Because I knew, one hundred percent, how much he wanted me. I knew how much I wanted him.

If he pulled me to him and kissed me right now, I wouldn't stop him, either.

"What are you doing over there?"

I looked over at Jake and blinked for a minute.

"Mellie?"

"Oh. Um, it's just stuff for an event. A couple are getting married in nine months and want to book basically the whole hotel. I'm trying to figure out if we can do it and give a group rate like they're requesting."

"How many people are there?"

"Enough to fill all but two rooms. The whole wedding party need to stay here, and it sounds like a huge hoopla."

"Like…a hundred people?"

"No, think Kim Kardashian when she married that basketball player."

"I know nothing about the Kardashians."

Of course, he didn't. "Big. Crazy. Enough to make me want to stab my eyeballs with a fork."

Jake laughed, but it sounded hollow to me. He didn't really mean it, which was good, because I didn't want him to mean it.

I turned back to my work without another word.

"Mellie?"

I tilted my face away from him and ignored him.

"Mellie. You can't ignore me forever."

"I can," I said.

Jake sighed and got up. Out of the corner of my eye, I watched him walk around the desk and come toward me. He gripped hold of my ankles and threw my bare feet to the floor, then tore the paperwork from me and threw it on the desk. "You can't ignore me," he said firmly. He leaned down and gripped the arms of my chair, bringing his face level with mine.

I sat up straight and glared at him. I folded my arms and kept up my hard stare.

"We can't ignore this," he said in a softer, lower voice. "And we're not going to. I'm not going to sit here in this fucking office with so much unsaid. We're going to talk about what happened, and if you don't want to talk, you're gonna damn well listen to what I have to say."

I set my jaw.

I didn't want to hear it, but that didn't matter.

"I'm sorry." He searched my gaze. "If Sam coming back is why you're so angry, then I'm sorry. He's a dick. Probably one of the most selfish people I know. He knew we were having dinner and—"

"It wasn't him!" I shoved at his arm, and surprisingly, he let me go. I got up off the chair and walked across the room, running my hands through my hair. "Jesus, I couldn't care less that he walked in. I'm more annoyed that we were in that situation to begin with."

"You're more annoyed we were kissing?"

"Yes!" I almost tore my hair out as I turned around. "Fucking hell, Jake. You're my boss! If Sam didn't come back, what would have happened, huh? We'd have gone further, and if we'd had sex, we never would have been able to come back from that."

"Has it occurred to you that maybe I don't want to come back from that?"

I rubbed my hands down my face. "We can't—we can't even get to that point!"

"Listen to me." He walked to me and cupped my face. I tried to get him off me, but he simply grabbed my face again and made me look at him. "I don't care. I don't care that I'm your boss. I like you. I like you a hell of a lot more than I should. I can't stop thinking about you."

"That doesn't make this right!"

"And being your boss doesn't make it wrong. If you can look me in the eye right now and tell me that you don't feel anything for me, that you never want me to touch you again, then fine. I'll let you go, and I'll do just that."

He searched my eyes. His gaze was dark and intense, and his fingers twitched against my cheeks.

My mouth was dry.

I wanted to say it. I wanted to rip the lie from my throat and tell him just that. I didn't feel anything, and I never wanted him to touch me again.

But, as he looked into my eyes, I felt everything. I felt stupid and desperate, heady and free. I wanted him to touch me harder, dig his fingers into my skin so I could really feel how bad he wanted me.

"Say it, Mellie. If you really feel that this is wrong, tell me that."

"I can't," I whispered, looking into his eyes. "I just...I can't tell you that."

His response was to kiss me. Softly, gently, just one simple touch that sent a shiver down my spine. "I like you. I really, really like you. I want you to understand that. I know this is awkward and not ideal, and I promise you it's nothing to do with the fact the first part of you I saw was your boobs."

I dropped my gaze and bit the inside of my cheek to hide my smile.

Jake slid one hand down and hooked two fingers under my chin, tilting my head back up. "I mean it." His smile was lopsided. "You're the clumsiest person I've ever met, but that also makes you the most adorable. And I'm not going to lie;

I'm starting to think I might be a little obsessed with you and your eccentricities."

"I'm not eccentric. I don't have eccentricities."

"The first times we met, you either showed me your boobs or smashed something."

"Don't forget when I hurt myself." I paused. I'd just bought into his narrative. "Damn it."

Jake laughed, wrapping his hand around the back of my neck. He pulled me in to kiss him again while still laughing, so I just pouted at him.

"We still need to talk about this. We need to talk about how it works." I pulled back from him and sat on the edge of the desk. Why was this such a comfortable position? "So, don't think we can just waltz into anything without discussing the steps first."

"Waltz into something. That would be a lot easier than this talking thing."

"We have to talk!"

"Of course, we do. You're a woman. You love to talk."

I put my hands on my hips. "Listen here. If I had my own way, I'd still be sitting in my chair, working, happily ignoring you."

"You were happy enough to eat the donuts I bought you."

"Well, duh. They're donuts. Everyone is happy to eat donuts."

He raised his eyebrows. "I'm not always happy to eat donuts."

I gasped, pressing my hand against my chest. "How can you not—you know, I'm starting to question my feelings for you after that. That might be treasonous."

"I don't need to eat donuts if I'm going to kiss you." He walked over to me, licked his fingertip, and pressed it to my cheek. "Because you're guaranteed to taste just like them." He turned his finger.

There was powdered sugar on it.

I licked my fingers and wiped at my cheek. I'd probably take off half the makeup I had on there, but I didn't want to be walking around with anything on my cheek.

Jake laughed. He brought his hands down to my knees and parted my thighs, stepping between them.

Thank God I'd worn a dress with a flirty skirt today. Parting one's legs in a pencil skirt would be a nightmare.

"So…Talking. Tonight?" Hope flickered in his eyes.

"For someone who doesn't want to talk, you're pretty keen on doing so."

He rested his hands on the tops of my thighs and leaned in. "I know, but I have an ulterior motive."

"Which is?"

He dipped his head. His lips ghosted along my jaw until his mouth found my ear. "The sooner we clear it up, the sooner we get to fuck."

My stomach flipped. "Um, well, I guess—that's a good reason, huh? Yep. Definitely."

His grin was so sexy it basically tugged on my clit. Not a good thing since he was standing between my legs, and if I made it too obvious, I didn't think he'd wait until tonight.

"Tonight." He brought his mouth back close to mine. "We're going to talk. We're going to figure it out. I'm going to cook—"

"Oh, dear God."

"—You're going to cook," he corrected himself.

I nodded. "Better. I don't need food poisoning."

"And when we're done, we'll go upstairs and we'll finish what we started last week."

"Upstairs? You're optimistic for a guy standing between my legs right now."

"You wanna do it now? I'm not fussy. I've got the worst case of fucking blue balls since I was thirteen and saw my first Playboy."

"Was it Sam's?" I deadpanned.

He cough-laughed. "Actually, yeah. Yeah, it was."

"Not surprised."

"So, tonight? It's a date?"

I blushed and held his gaze for a second. "It's a date."

He grinned, then leaned forward and kissed me. It took him only seconds to deepen the kiss to something more, and my fingers quickly found their way to his shirt and grabbed on tight.

Knock. Knock. Knock.

Jake pulled back, groaning. "Why is it that every time I kiss you, I'm interrupted?"

I shrugged as he stepped away from me. "Because your cousin is an ass, and right now, you should be working?"

He stared at me. "You should be working, too."

"I was until you made me stop."

"Spitfire? Shut up and work."

I flipped him the bird, ignoring his stupid grinning face, and sat back down while he went to see whoever was on the other side of the door.

If we were going to see each other, we really needed separate offices, or I had the feeling he'd never let me get anything done.

TWENTY-TWO

UPSIDE #22: YOU NEVER HAVE TO WORRY ABOUT WHETHER OR NOT YOU NEED TO SEND FANCY PHOTO CHRISTMAS CARDS. WHICH I MIGHT NOW HAVE TO DO. CRAP.

If I'd learned anything from meeting Jake, it was that my self-control was practically minimal.

I mean, I knew that anyway. That was how I'd ended up flashing him in the very first place—my inability to say no to cocktails and to tell my friends where to stick it.

There were worse things to have no self-control over. I mean, kissing Jacob Creed wasn't a bad thing, it turned out. The man could kiss, even if he did keep getting interrupted.

And aside from his apartment, he'd been kissing me at stupid times, anyway.

It really was all his fault he kept getting interrupted.

I finished drying my hair and set the blow dryer down on my bed. My hair was now fluffy, but I couldn't be bothered to get the straightening iron out. Besides, this might have been a date, but it wasn't really.

We didn't need to get to know each other. We didn't need to see each other at our best, because we'd already spent so much time together, it didn't really matter at all.

I did, however, put a lick of mascara over my lashes, do a little to fill in my brows, and powder my face. I needed to look somewhat human, after all.

I tugged my jeans up at the back and headed downstairs. Since I'd learned that Jake was almost always early—frustrating for someone who was late for everything except work—I was glad I'd left work a little early to make sure I could cook properly.

Since he'd mentioned wanting to cook jambalaya, I'd cooked one myself and had it simmering in my skillet while I'd showered. I wanted it ready for when he showed up, because I knew that as soon as we were done talking, there'd be no chance of eating.

So, the plan was to eat first.

It was a pretty good plan, if you asked me. Nobody had, but nobody needed to, after all.

I stirred the jambalaya right as there was two knocks at the door. I swallowed hard, putting the spoon on the kitchen counter.

I almost hesitated before I opened the door, but that was only because I was nervous.

I knew where this night would lead.

I mean, it had better lead to sex like he promised.

I wasn't wearing matching underwear for no reason.

"Hi," I said a little too breathlessly.

"You usually open the door before you greet someone," he said from the other side of the door.

And just like that, we were back to normal.

I opened the door with a pout. "I see normal service is being resumed."

"If by normal service you mean you're a klutz, then yes." He grinned, stepping inside and holding up a bottle of wine. "And judging by how nervous you look, it's a good thing I stopped for this on the way over here."

"I'm not nervous."

"Tell that to your eyes, spitfire. You look like you're about to lose your virginity." He turned and eyed me. "Wait. You're not a virgin, are you?"

"If I didn't think you were joking…" I pushed the door shut.

"You'd hit me, right?"

"Right."

He came back over from the kitchen and locked my front door. "Where's your phone?"

I jerked my head between the door and him. "Why did you lock the door? And why do you need my phone?"

"Because, when we're done talking, I don't want to be interrupted. I'd hate for someone to call or stop by when my cock is inside you."

Well. That was an excellent point.

"Um, my phone is by the stove." My gaze flicked from the door to him. "Is your phone off?"

"Off and in my car," he replied. "Mostly because I took great pleasure in telling Sam that the orange juice he and his guest drank out of this morning was the one I opened."

"I don't understand why that's pleasurable to you at all."

His grin was playful but also devilish. "I didn't use a glass."

I wrinkled up my face as I moved to the stove. "That's gross. But, he totally deserved it."

"If I'd been there for ten more seconds, he'd have punched me." Jake pulled two wine glasses out of the cupboard. "Seriously—I already pissed him off last night by telling him he should worry more about his own fleeting relationships than what I'm doing, so the juice thing was the cherry on the top. He's borderline OCD, so he's probably scrubbing his mouth out with bleach right now."

"You guys had a fight?" I looked over my shoulder.

"Not really. His apology to me for interrupting us was bullshit, so I called him on it. It's not my fault he lives his life like a college bachelor and not an adult with responsibilities. Until he does that, he doesn't get to lecture me on dating you."

"We're dating?" I turned around like I'd been hit by lightning, and my grip on the spoon weakened.

The spoon clattered to the floor, splashing sauce everywhere.

Jake was halfway through uncorking the wine, and he froze to look down at the spoon. "I was about to say yes, but I'm not really sure how you'll take that answer right now."

I bent down for the spoon and turned to the sink. "I mean, I thought we were talking about it. It's presumptuous, don't you think? What if we decide this is a bad idea?"

"We already know this is a bad idea, but no great story ever started with someone saying they had a good idea. If they did, you'd never have flashed me that night."

"No, correction." I turned and pointed the now-clean spoon at him. "Most great stories start with "I have a great idea!" except the idea is almost always a dreadful one."

"Fine. No great story ever started with a good idea that didn't turn out to be a bad one."

"There we go." I gave the food one last stir and grabbed a wet cloth to clean the floor.

Jake popped the wine with a tiny pop-hiss from the bottle. "Kind of like how we met. I bet you were told it was a good idea."

"How did you know?" I drawled, pulling two plates down.

"Because, in hindsight, it really was a dreadful idea." He poured the wine, then put the bottle in my fridge like it was his own.

Dear God. Is this what dating felt like? It'd been a long-ass time since I'd done that.

And why was this so very comfortable for him to just stroll in and pour wine?

Aside from the fact it was wine, of course.

I turned off the stove and dished up my latest creation. Jake was already sitting at my kitchen table when I turned around, so I set one plate in front of him and the other opposite him for me. After grabbing cutlery and passing some to him with a smile, I took my seat, and we both started eating.

We were only a few mouthfuls in when he started speaking.

"This is good," he said.

"Thanks." I smiled and looked down at my plate.

"So. What worries you about us dating?"

I choked on some rice. I banged my fist against my chest, and through my watery eyes, I could see a chuckling Jake get up and get me a glass of water.

"Here. Can we finish the conversation before you die on me?"

I took a long drink from the water and wiped my eyes with my finger. "Um, wow, that came out of nowhere."

"Not really. The entire point of tonight's conversation is to talk through our relationship, so I thought I'd start."

"You could have given a girl a heads up!" I had some more water. My throat hurt now.

Jake looked at me for a moment, holding his wine glass. "Okay, here. Let's talk about us."

"Can I have a minute?"

"Spitfire, if I had my way, we'd go straight to the fucking. You're the one who wants to talk. I'm pretty damn sure we're not having sex until we've talked about this, so do a man a favor and get on with it. Especially if you're going to wear jeans that tight."

Were my jeans tight? I didn't know. They were just...jeans.

"I know you're worried about us seeing each other." He stabbed his fork into a piece of sausage. "So, talk to me about it."

I set my fork down and sipped my wine. This sucked. I might have been the one who said we had to talk, but that didn't mean I was good talking about my feelings.

Hello. I ran a hotel while my best friends handled the feelings stuff. I'd had a chance to go into business with Peyton for Pick-A-Dick, but I'd turned it down.

"My biggest concern is how we handle it at work," I admitted. "It's already awkward with you coming in and changing some things. And, let's be honest, it's been two weeks. We've spent a lot of time together, but it's not really long enough to be the basis of a serious relationship."

He nodded slowly. "I happen to agree with you there. That said, the solution is simple. We do our best to keep our private relationship away from work until we know for sure that it'll all work out."

"You don't think it'll work out?"

"I didn't say that. But you can imagine how uncomfortable the staff would be if we were suddenly in a relationship after two weeks. Besides—they don't need to know. It's not their business."

"Them being uncomfortable is what I'm worried about."

"Hey, it's okay." He put down his fork and leaned forward, reaching across the table to squeeze my hand. "Really. We don't have to tell anyone anything while we're still figuring it out ourselves."

My lips curved to a smile. "Good. But that means we have to keep it completely away from work, and you haven't been very good at that so far."

"I can keep it separate. But that might mean I'm going to spend a lot of time here. With you. Naked."

"I've had worse offers."

"Sound a little bit more enthusiastic, would you?"

I clapped my hands together and squealed. "Oh, yay!"

"Now, you're just being a pain in my ass."

"On the bright side," I said, picking my fork back up. "The clumsiest thing I've done today is drop a spoon."

Jake paused. "You almost knocked over the lamp in our office."

"It was in my way."

"You threw the office phone at it."

I sighed. "I didn't throw it at the lamp. I threw it in the direction of the lamp. It's not my fault the person on the other end was stupid or that the lamp was in the phone's way."

"You have excuses for everything."

"No, I have a reason for everything. There's a big difference."

"Is there a reason we're still sitting at this table, and you're not naked on your bed?"

I blinked at him. "Yes. We're talking about our relationship."

Jake sipped his wine. "I feel like, right now, we've talked enough."

"I don't think so."

He stood up and walked around the table. My gaze followed him like he was something shiny, and I was a goddamn magpie. He grabbed hold of my hands and yanked me up. My thigh grazed the table, and if it'd hit any harder, it would have knocked something off.

Crisis one: averted.

Jake wrapped his arms around me and pulled me close to him. "We can talk more later. We can figure it out. Right now, I want you."

"My—my dinner is getting cold."

"Are you nervous?"

"No."

He raised his eyebrows.

"A little," I admitted. "I've never planned sex. It usually happens spontaneously."

"I can do spontaneous."

"This is already—"

He bent down and, grabbing me by the thighs, picked me up and hauled me over his shoulder. I screamed and grabbed hold of him, equal parts scared and impressed by his strength.

"Bedroom?"

"Upstairs."

"Really? I thought we were going down."

"Jake."

"Which door, Mellie?" he demanded, stopping at the top of the stairs. "This one?"

He opened the door to my messy closet. "Definitely not."

"Not that there was ever a mood," I said. "But, you're killing it a little. It's the next door." I pointed to my bedroom.

He opened the door to my room and hauled me inside. "There was a mood. There was a very fucking good mood last night before we were interrupted."

"I know that, but now it's awkward."

"You're the awkward one here, spitfire. All I keep thinking is how quickly I can turn you on as much as I did last night."

To be honest, that was a test I was interested in.

He slid me down his body until my feet touched the ground in front of my bed. One hand went to the back of my neck; the other clamped around my waist. "I already know your neck is sensitive," he murmured, dipping his head and brushing his lips against my neck.

That was unfair.

"And you like it when I kiss it, even though you pretend you don't," he continued, kissing my neck a few more times. Short, hot, soft kisses that made me squirm against him.

This was definitely playing dirty.

"So, I'm pretty sure you're already on your way there," he said right into my ear. He kissed along my jaw until he reached the corner of my mouth. "And if not, you're about to be."

He kissed me before I could respond. And he didn't go in slow.

He kissed me hard, almost ruthlessly. It felt so damn good I couldn't fight him, I couldn't dispute it. All I could do was grab hold of his shirt and kiss him back just as hard.

It was like all the things I'd felt for him in the past several days all came to a head. The lust burst through my veins. Desire rippled across my skin, and shivers came out of nowhere until I was practically trembling in his arms.

My lungs were tight and my heart was fast and everything tingled. The passion I felt in his kiss and his touch was more than enough to turn me on at a lightning speed.

He broke the kiss, pushing me back to the bed. He tore his t-shirt over his head and threw it to the floor before he covered my body with his and kissed me again. My fingers went wild, tracing a map of invisible lines across his back.

My back arched, my hips moved, and my nails scratched as his kiss got deeper and deeper.

He stopped. Yanked me up. Pulled off my shirt. I didn't care. It didn't matter. Not as it fell to the floor or as I wrapped my arms around his neck.

I wanted him.

I wanted him as he moved down the bed, his lips doing the same to my body. Down my neck, across the dip of my collarbone—over the swell of my tits. He even flicked his tongue out, teasing me as my body reacted to him as if it was made to do so.

His hands reached the waistband of my jeans, and he pulled them down my legs oh-so-slowly, peeling the material away from my skin until my legs were free. He did the same with his own jeans, except his fell a lot quicker than mine.

My eyes fell to his cock. Hard and thick, the outline of it against his bright-red boxer briefs was obvious. My tongue flicked out to wet my lips, and as I met his eyes, pure desire shone back at me, but his smile was wolfish and sexy.

It was only seconds before he was back over me, kissing me, but this time, he was between my legs.

My legs bent at the knee, teasing wrapping around his body. His cock already pressed firm against my clit, and bursts of heat kept flying through my body like I was about to combust.

He didn't speak—he didn't need to. Neither did I. All I needed was the crazy rush of having our almost-naked bodies together.

I needed our totally naked bodies together.

Brazenly, I reached down and grabbed the waistband of his boxers. He grinned against my lips and whispered, "Condom?"

Oh. Shit. Did I have a freaking condom?

Jake laughed, dropping his forehead to my shoulder. "I got it."

I relaxed, throwing my forearm over my eyes. Thank God one of us was prepared.

We both knew it wouldn't be me.

He got up and retrieved a condom from the pocket of his jeans. I watched—with way too much enthusiasm—as he kicked off his underwear, opened the condom, and positioned it at the end of his cock.

My eyes followed his fingers as they rolled it on. I squirmed, the wetness between my legs uncomfortable thanks to the silky material of my panties. Jake's eyes dropped to the apex of my thighs, and I knew he saw that I couldn't sit still.

He leaned back over me, practically stalking me, and slid his hand down my side. He hooked his thumb in the side of my panties and pulled them down, straightening to get the other side down, too.

Discarded on the floor, he parted my legs and settled himself between them. This time, there was no delay in me wrapping my legs around his toned waist. The only thing that stopped him kissing me straight away was the unhooking of my bra.

He didn't even pull it off. He simply undid the clasp between my breasts and let the cups fall to the side before his lips recaptured mine.

One hand slid between us slightly awkwardly. His fingers glided through the wetness of my pussy, rubbing over my clit a few times before he apparently decided I was wet enough to take him.

Slow.

That was how he entered me. The polar opposite from the way he'd kissed me just minutes ago. Slow and easy, he allowed me to adjust and take him as I wanted to.

Heat sparked through me. There was nothing like the way he felt as he slowly moved inside me. Nothing felt as good as the slow, easy strokes of his cock inside me and the slow, gentle way his lips played with mine.

My fingers wound in his hair. His dug into my ass cheek, holding me in place, and his other hand was flat on the bed and holding him steady over me.

Slowly, the heat built in me.

Slowly, he moved faster, thrusting his hips with a wild pace that was scarily comfortable for me.

I was getting lost. Lost in his kiss, his scent, his touch. Lost in how it felt to be so close to him, to be so intimate with someone.

I didn't know how it happened. I didn't know how I went from coherence to nothing, from the easy build of pleasure to the fireworks of an orgasm that flooded through every little bit of my body.

I went limp as he gripped my ass and little tighter. The tell-tale stillness and tensing accompanied by a low groan told me he'd joined me in ecstasy. He relaxed over me pretty quickly, somehow managing to not suffocate me, and kissed the side of my neck.

"Told you I could create the mood," he murmured against my skin.

"Shhh," I whispered, tapping him with one finger. "Catching my breath."

He laughed and pulled out of me, rolling to the side to remove the condom. I pointed in the vague area of the plastic trashcan I kept next to my vanity before my arm flopped back down onto the bed.

I didn't know how he was able to move.

I was ready to curl up for a nap.

"I'm hungry," he said. "Can you reheat jambalaya?"

I forced my eyes open and half-glared at him. "How can you think of food in a time like this?"

"In a time like what? You're post-orgasm, spitfire. You're not post-apocalypse."

"Speak for yourself," I muttered. Groaning, I forced myself to roll and sit up. "I was hoping for a nap."

He took my hands in his and pulled me up onto my wobbly legs, skin glistening with sweat. "Food, nap, more sex?" He didn't wait for me to answer before he said, "Yeah. Food, nap, more sex."

He let go of my hands, and unfortunately for me, my legs were still like jelly, and I wasn't prepared for having to stand up with my own strength.

I fell back onto the bed with an "oomph." "That's not how this—" I tried to call after him, but one very naked Jacob Creed had already left my room and was on his way down the stairs.

I stared at his peachy ass as it disappeared before shrugging and lying back down.

He could get the food.

I'd take the nap…

Until later, apparently.

EPILOGUE

Two weeks later.

UPSIDE #23: DON'T ASK ME. I'M NOT SINGLE. I RAN OUT OF IDEAS.

"This is bullshit." Peyton paced back and forth across her office.

"The fact I'm here and not having a nice lunch with my girlfriend? I agree," Jake said, sitting back on the bright-purple sofa.

She glared at him.

I kicked him. "Peyt, you walked into the challenge. You know Dom's the romantic of the two of you."

Yeah, I didn't really understand that, either.

"That's not the point. The point is that my brother challenged me to be the one to prove him wrong. Why can't he do it himself?" she ranted, still going back and forth. "It's his stupid argument, not mine. I already know you can screw a person three times and not fall in love."

Jake opened his mouth to say something, and I elbowed him.

We weren't there yet. Even though we'd definitely done it more than three times, and I was pretty sure I was in love with him. Almost. Pretty much. Was there a scale for that?

"I don't want to sleep with someone three times!" Peyton shouted.

"Is once your limit?" Jake asked.

Peyton pointed at me. "Control your human."

I pinched the bridge of my nose. She needed her own human. For more than one night…

I rested my hand on Jake's thigh. "Why don't you grab lunch and take it back to the office? Chloe will be back in a couple minutes. No offense, but you being here isn't helping."

That, and those two were struggling to find a common ground to forge a friendship. Not that it was hard. Peyton struggled with that in general, because she struggled with a little thing called being nice.

Jake glanced at Peyton one last time before turning to me. "Okay. 'Cause if I stay here any longer, I'm gonna climb onto the roof and take the outdoor elevator down to the sidewalk."

I kissed him quickly and gave him a shove. He stopped to kiss me once more, ignoring Peyton's vomiting sound, before leaving without saying goodbye to her.

If she could have, I swear she would have slammed the door behind him.

It was exhausting.

"What am I going to do?" she asked me, finally stopping her pacing.

"Tell Dom no," I said, giving her the most obvious answer. "You don't have to prove anything, Peyt."

"Tell him no?" Her voice was getting higher and higher. "Let him win?"

Oh, good. Their sibling rivalry was so fun.

"Hell no!"

The door swung open, and Chloe shuffled in. "Sorry, sorry! The traffic was awful. Here's your…double shot hurricane you asked for," she added warily, handing Chloe a huge cocktail cup.

Oh, good. She was day drinking. That was always fun when she needed a nap in the afternoon.

It also meant she was really, really distressed by this challenge her brother had issued her.

"Dom filled me in," Chloe said, taking the seat next to me that Jake had just left. "I told him he was fucking dumb. We all know you can screw someone three times and not fall in love. I told him to stop sharing your mom's Netflix account and watching her stupid emotional movies."

"Thank you!" Peyton threw her arm in the air at him. "And he'll pick the guy I get to screw based on who's in my database? That's bullshit!"

Chloe grimaced.

"It actually is." I glanced at Peyton before looking at Chloe. "I mean, he's the dater. He literally creates relationships. He's not going to pick the guy she can screw, he's going to pick the guy he thinks is most compatible for her."

"I know that," Chloe replied. "He'll probably pull someone from our database over just to screw with her."

"Noooooo!" she moaned, sitting in the armchair next to us. She literally sank into the cushions of the chair.

I loved her office. It was so plush and comfy.

"Why don't we do it?" Chloe sat up straight. "I mean, think about it, Peyt. We're on your side. We agree with you. We'll pick a guy we know you'll never fall for, and Dom can't argue, because we're impartial. We're not involved in this stupid bet."

"Yeah, well, you better make me win. I don't want to lose five hundred bucks to that idiot," Peyton huffed.

"You bet five hundred bucks?" I sputtered out. "Why?"

"Because! I need to be right, and if I win, he'll go away."

Chloe and I shared a look. "Sure," she said slowly. "Come on, Peyt. You don't have to prove him wrong, and you get to win. Let us do it for you."

"You know we're right," I added.

Peyton rubbed her hand over her face, sighed, and looked at us. "You know what? Fine. What's the worst that could happen?"

Well, there was something to be said for famous last words.

I hoped like hell she wouldn't end up eating them...

THE END

THE HOOK-UP EXPERIMENT, Peyton's story, is coming March 13th and is available for pre-order everywhere now.

Visit
www.emmahart.org/the-hook-up-experiment
for more.

THE HOOK-UP EXPERIMENT

1. Hate-screw my high school nemesis.
2. Remember to hate him.
3. Prove my brother wrong.
It should be simple.
It isn't.

As the owner of hook-up website Pick-A-Dick, my job is simple. Connect two people for a no-strings, no-expectations hook-up. The plus for my clients? I'm the one who gets to sift through the dick pics.
Except this time, the dick pics are required.
The only problem is that my brother—who co-owns Pick-A-D*ck's sister dating website—doesn't believe in my business. He doesn't think you can hook up with someone three times and not fall in love.
My best friend—his business partner—disagrees with him. Which is how I end up being challenged to find the answer.
And that's how I find myself reconnecting with my high-school nemesis, Elliot Sloane. The guy who asked me to junior prom then stood me up. The guy who egged my car when I rejected him the second time. The guy who convinced my senior homecoming date to ghost me.
Three hook-ups. Even I can deal with that, especially since I know he is packing in the pants department, and I know this experiment only has one outcome.
It should be easy to hate-screw the guy who made my high school years a living nightmare, but he's not that person anymore. He's a hot-as-hell single dad, working as a builder to make ends' meet, fighting for custody of his daughter.
And, maybe, just maybe, I was wrong...

ABOUT THE AUTHOR

Emma Hart is the New York Times and USA TODAY bestselling author of over thirty novels and has been translated into several different languages.

She is a mother, wife, lover of wine, Pink Goddess, and valiant rescuer of wild baby hedgehogs.

Emma prides herself on her realistic, snarky smut, with comebacks that would make a PMS-ing teenage girl proud.

Yes, really. She's that sarcastic.

You can find her online at:
www.emmahart.org
www.facebook.com/emmahartbooks
www.instagram.com/EmmaHartAuthor
www.pinterest.com/authoremmahart

Alternatively, you can join her reader group at http://bit.ly/EmmaHartsHartbreakers.

You can also get all things Emma to your email inbox by signing up for Emma Alerts*. http://bit.ly/EmmaAlerts

*Emails sent for sales, new releases, pre-order availability, and cover reveals. Each cover reveal contains an exclusive excerpt.

BOOKS BY EMMA HART

The Vegas Nights series:
Sin
Lust

Stripped series:
Stripped Bare
Stripped Down

The Burke Brothers:
Dirty Secret
Dirty Past
Dirty Lies
Dirty Tricks
Dirty Little Rendezvous

The Holly Woods Files:
Twisted Bond
Tangled Bond
Tethered Bond
Tied Bond
Twirled Bond
Burning Bond
Twined Bond

By His Game series:
Blindsided
Sidelined
Intercepted

Call series:
Late Call
Final Call
His Call

Wild series:
Wild Attraction
Wild Temptation
Wild Addiction
Wild: The Complete Series

The Game series:
The Love Game
Playing for Keeps
The Right Moves
Worth the Risk

Memories series:
Never Forget
Always Remember

Standalones:
Blind Date
Being Brooke
Catching Carly
Casanova
Mixed Up
Miss Fix-It
Miss Mechanic
The Upside to Being Single
The Hook-Up Experiment (coming March 13, 2018)
The Dating Experiment (coming May 8, 2018)

Made in the USA
San Bernardino, CA
02 November 2018